Crazy about Alaska

Alaska Dream Romances

Falling for Alaska

Loving Alaska

Merrying in Alaska
(A Christmas Novella)

Crazy about Alaska

Alaska Matchmakers Romances

Accidentally Matched

Finally Matched

Hopefully Matched

Merrily Matched
(A Christmas Novella)

Surprisingly Matched

By Shannon L. Brown

Crime-Solving Cousins Mysteries

(For ages 8-12)

The Feather Chase

The Treasure Key

The Chocolate Spy

Crazy about Alaska

AN ALASKA DREAM ROMANCE

CATHRYN BROWN

Sienna Bay Press

Sienna Bay Press
PO Box 158582
Nashville, Tennessee 37215

www.shannonlbrown.com

Cover Designed by Najla Qamber Designs
(www.najlaqamberdesigns.com)

Book Layout ©2015 BookDesignTemplates.com

Publisher's Note: This is a work of fiction. Names, characters, places, and incidents are a product of the author's imagination. Locales and public names are sometimes used for atmospheric purposes. Any resemblance to actual people, living or dead, or to businesses, companies, events, institutions, or locales is completely coincidental.

Previously published as a book by Shannon L. Brown.

Crazy About Alaska/Cathryn Brown

ISBN: 978-1-945527-23-4

To Jean,
No matter how many times you left Alaska,
it always called you back.

You've always been more of a big sister than an aunt.
I hope we have many more shopping trips together.

You love crossword puzzles so in your honor,
there's one on my website about this series.

Chapter One

Holly Harris grabbed the edge of the porch's roof as her foot slipped off her makeshift stool. She tried to lower herself back to the window ledge she'd used as the last step in her mighty plan to climb onto the roof. Her foot missed the ledge and hit the high back of the chair she'd stacked on top of a trunk—her first and second steps—instead. The heavy chair moved and, a moment later, hit the lawn with a dull thud.

Grabbing onto a rib on the metal roof, she held on for dear life. Using every one of the mom-muscles she'd developed while carrying twins in her arms, she wrestled herself inch by inch onto the porch roof.

"Be a real estate agent." Holly pulled harder. "You'll," she gasped, "like it." She dragged herself onto the forest-green roof, wincing as the textured steel dug into her right side. One slip-on shoe slipped off, landing soundlessly on the grass below, confirming the fact that she would too if she loosened her grip. A fierce tug later, she'd managed to get her upper body on the roof, but her lower half still dangled off the eight-or-nine-foot drop. Breath coming in gasps, she rested and waited for her heart rate to slow to something that didn't signal an imminent call for paramedics.

"Sure. I *love* my work," she muttered.

When she'd sucked in enough oxygen for her brain to kick in again, she realized she had a couple of problems. Her cell phone sat directly beneath her on the porch itself, and—like it or not—she couldn't return the way she'd come. If the window that overlooked the roof wasn't unlocked, she'd have to shout for help. Jemma and Bree always said she was the boldest of the three sisters. She'd gotten in trouble many times for leaping before she looked as a kid, and still hadn't learned the lesson.

Pulling with her remaining strength, she brought all but her lower legs onto the roof. "Chocolate. I *need* chocolate." With none dropping from heaven, she continued, reached for another metal rib on the roof and kicked her legs, sending her other shoe flying.

"Ouch!" a male voice said.

Holly tugged herself up the rest of the way and perched on the nearly flat roof. She caught a glimpse of a blond-headed man rubbing the top of his head while he darted onto the porch.

"You must be the world's worst burglar. Broad daylight. I will say in your favor that most houses in this neighborhood are empty in the middle of a weekday." The voice sounded familiar.

"I'll have you know that I'm a real estate agent." She paused. That didn't explain a moment of her crazy morning. "I have the owner's permission."

"To scale their porch?"

2

"Actually, yes. The owners listed the house with me, and accidentally locked the key inside before leaving town."

Silence greeted her. The man, with nicely trimmed hair, leaned over the porch railing to admire her now defunct step stool—the box and chair. "You could have been injured." Each word he spoke made him sound more familiar, but the twinge of memory didn't bring a happy sensation.

"This has occurred to me. Listen, I may need your help getting back down if this window isn't unlocked." Holly crawled over to it and kneeled with one knee on either side of a metal roof rib. She tugged upward on the window sill, but nothing happened. With her heart rate ramping up again and a rescue with sirens blaring feeling all too close, she held onto the window frame and rose to her feet to get better leverage. This time when she pulled, the window slid up a few inches. Working it upward bit by bit, she was soon rewarded with an opening large enough to squeeze through.

"The window's open, so I can get inside. You don't need to stay any longer. Thank you!"

Holly slid through headfirst. Utter chaos stretched in front of her—something she'd never allowed with her five-year-old twins, but not unexpected in what she knew to be a ten-year-old boy's room. After rising to her feet, she brushed herself off, pleased she didn't find any clothing damage. Then she picked her way through a demolition derby of toy trucks and cars along with other boys' toys, being careful not to step on anything in her stocking feet.

She followed the mess out the door to discover that it continued down the hall. Pink and purple toys suitable for a girl two years younger than the boy littered the space, along with clothing and a wadded-up set of bed sheets. The whole family must have set things to the side in their rush to leave. Holly walked to the top of the stairs, which overlooked the open living area below.

More toys and other bits of daily life were scattered about. She felt a scream rise in her throat. Hands on her chest, she willed herself to stay in control, so only a whimper escaped. "I'm a real estate professional. I can handle this. Think about the day you'll close on this house and the check they'll hand you." She stood tall. "Holly Harris, you aren't a quitter." Dreading what she'd uncover downstairs, she added, "Or a screamer. Remember that."

Nodding once, she took the first of the steps down, then another, the mess on the ground level growing closer with each second. A plate with bread still on it sat on the table; what appeared to be tomato sauce splashed the pots on the stove; cupboards stood open. She knew she'd find a sink full of dishes; that's how her day had gone, and she really didn't like to do dishes. She'd have to clear it all out to sell the house.

The lockbox with the key inside sat on the dining room table, right where the owners thought they'd left it. If they'd hung it on the doorknob before they'd driven away, her tryout for the circus high-wire act wouldn't have been necessary. She gleefully unlocked the front door and went out the easy way. As she latched it around the outside knob, she smiled. One problem solved. Now, she could use the combination lock—numbers she knew because she'd provided the device—to get inside at any time.

"I guess you really are a real estate agent."

She jerked her head up, staring into sky-blue eyes she recognized from two tortuous college English classes. "Professor O'Connell?" She'd had trouble keeping her focus on the lecture and off the handsome lecturer during the first week of class. How could you take notes when your heart raced, and silly grins kept popping onto your face? Any positive emotions had ceased when she'd received her first graded assignment—one that had stomped all over her dreams of writing books.

"Holly Harris? I thought you were an elementary education major. Why this?" He pointed at the porch roof.

Standing, she sighed. "When I didn't get a teaching position right away, I became a real estate agent. I liked the idea of paying my bills."

"I hadn't realized you'd graduated already." He held out his hands, a navy-blue shoe in each. "It's quite a change from teaching. Has this profession worked out well?"

Not today, she thought as she took the shoes and bent over to put them back on her feet. She'd chosen her footwear this morning to coordinate with navy pants and a red sweater, not knowing any of them would be worn during an adventure. "I've closed on quite a few properties, so it's become steady income." Except for the lull she was experiencing right now, but she had no plans to share that tidbit with him. Straightening, she gave him her best professional smile, the one she'd used in the photo on her business cards.

He leaned to his left to see around her and through the front door. "I've never heard of a need to break into a house in order to sell it. Is that a test the homeowners needed you to perform before signing?" A grin lit up his face, making him seem like a normal guy, not an uptight professor, reminding her that he couldn't have been more than five or six years older than her.

"They weren't supposed to leave until *after* I'd arrived. The family fell on hard times when Mr. Jackson lost his job late last year, but he found one in Colorado. They needed to sell their house—"

"And that's where you, with your unique climbing skills, came in."

She smiled slowly. "Yes. A friend of a friend recommended me to them. I got a wake-up call from Beaver Creek this morning telling me that they'd finished packing the car last night, so they decided to leave early. That makes them a day's drive from Palmer—or, I guess, a night's drive—by now."

"So you almost killed yourself for the sale."

"Pretty much sums it up." She noticed that the driveway held only her car, and no vehicle was parked in front of the house. "Do you live nearby?"

"Yes and no. I'm temporarily staying with a colleague. *Very* temporarily." He rubbed a hand over his face. "This house is going to be a hard sell. The owners left what looks like a crime scene."

Holly laughed. "I know. I'm pretty sure that the paint, carpet, and other flooring are in decent shape, though. The family just gave up and left a mess. I'll drag my two sisters over here along with one's husband and the other's fiancé tomorrow, and we'll get it cleaned up. I hope to finish by the end of that day."

Her words met a long pause. Just as it started to become uncomfortable, Dr. O'Connell said, "Nice to see you." His gaze lingered on her longer than she expected. Then he gave a small wave and cut across the lawn to the street.

There went the toughest professor she'd ever had. When she'd talked to him after class one day, and he'd stiffly answered her question, she'd also determined him to be one of the most boring individuals who'd ever walked the earth.

She couldn't come up with a single thing he and Matt, the man she was dating, had in common—other than the fact that they were males of the same species. An Alaska State Trooper, Matt treated her well and never criticized. Now if he'd just consistently answer calls or texts.

Eyeing the weighty chair she'd dragged off the porch and had somehow managed to lift onto the wooden trunk, she decided to wait for one of her sisters to help move them. Her muscles had had their workout for the day.

She grabbed her phone, punched in first Jemma's then Bree's numbers, and set up a time with each of them to help her the next day. Bree's fiancé was working on a business project, but Jemma's husband Nathaniel could come and handle the heavy lifting, and he offered to have his brother come for a short time too. *Thank goodness for family.* She'd put the men on garage duty after they'd cleared out the furniture in the house. If they had time and energy left.

With her phone halfway to her purse, she stopped. It didn't seem fair to let her family become involved in this disaster of a house without a heads-up. She snapped a photo with her phone and sent it off to each sister.

As she stood in the doorway, working out a plan of attack, a siren in the distance broke the morning's hush. She knew Matt wouldn't be involved in the event since he'd been sent to a village in the Bush—remote Alaska, unconnected by roads. A motorcycle came to life a block or two away and drove off. Then, silence. Now, she'd have a quiet day to herself. Too bad she couldn't spend it with her girls or writing.

She spun on her heels. Work called.

Chapter Two

Adam cruised down the Glenn Highway toward Anchorage, his motorcycle quickly eating up the miles on the hour-long ride. The sun danced in and out of clouds on this perfect July day.

He hadn't expected to see Holly Harris again. When she'd been his student, he'd wanted to ask her out. But being only a decade older than regular college students, and a few years older than adults like Holly who came back to finish their degrees, he'd made a policy he'd never broken: don't date any active students. It could go wrong in so many ways. He'd been on his best behavior, even more formal and proper with her than others, so he wouldn't accidentally slip up.

Holly wasn't a student anymore. That was the best news he'd had in a while. Should he follow up on his interest in the formerly off-limits student, or leave the past behind? Once this house hunt was over, he'd have peace and quiet enough to figure it out. Adam whistled a happy tune as he passed Chugiak, then Eagle River.

Today he hoped to find his new home; it was day nineteen of his house hunt. Dennis, his real estate agent, said he had several places to look at this afternoon. It would be an improvement to their working relationship if the man finally understood what his customer wanted. They were 0–10 so far. Condo. No. Townhouse. No. Tiny backyard. No!

He needed an agent who listened. Holly's image came to mind. If he hadn't committed to working with Dennis—a fellow professor's brother—he'd have given her a call. A stressful morning in his temporary digs had sent him on a walk around the area. Seeing a woman dangling precariously from a roof had him racing over to help, but she'd dragged herself to safety. Fear had turned to amusement after she'd climbed through the window. No one could question Holly's loyalty to her customers.

Adam pulled into a grocery store's parking lot when he reached the city and took out his phone to verify the address of the first house where he was supposed to meet Dennis. He memorized the route and took off, pulling into the driveway about fifteen minutes later.

As he cut the engine, he leaned back in the seat. He'd asked for a house with land around it, not one where it felt like the neighbor sat so close that the two homeowners could reach out their windows and shake hands. This one had more land than the townhouse he'd seen earlier in the week, but not much more.

Dennis stood smiling near the front door. "Adam, so good to see you." He gestured widely at the house. "I believe I've found exactly what you're looking for."

Unlikely, unless there's a stunning mountain view out the back and a moose grazing beside a pond.

Dennis eagerly pushed open the door and gestured his client inside. As soon as Adam crossed the threshold, he knew the house was a clean miss. Touring it, he tried to nod at the right moments. When they were done, Dennis locked up, and Adam followed him to the next house—one which turned out to be better as far as lot size went. The kitchen, with its chipped countertops and ancient appliances, was so tiny the two of them could barely fit into it. They crossed that place off the list and drove to house number three.

This time, Dennis had hit a home run. The substantial lot held a dozen birch trees. A robin scavenged on the ground beside one of them, adding to the peacefulness. They were in a typical suburban subdivision, but maybe it could work. As Adam moved down the sidewalk toward his agent, who'd once again hurried to open the front door, he said, "Dennis, excellent choice. It's peaceful and—" An airliner came into view and passed overhead, low enough that he could read the company's name on the side.

"I was about to mention that we're near the airport."

Adam put out his hand, and Dennis took it warily. "I'm sorry to have pulled you away from your other customers. I need to step back from this search right now. Thank you." Adam hurried over to his motorcycle. A final glance as he drove away showed his stunned former real estate agent standing on the doorstep, arm still partly outstretched.

Adam's life had become chaotic almost three weeks earlier when the only home he'd had in Anchorage—the one he'd quickly rented when he'd accepted a teaching position there—had gone up in smoke. Parties over the weekend were the norm in the townhouse attached to his unit's right side, but this time the renters next door had upped the excitement by adding grilled food to their dinner menu.

Too much lighter fluid squirted onto the charcoal grill on the deck had sent flames up and out, beginning the swift destruction of that unit and an onslaught of fire, smoke, and water damage to his. Nothing, not even his car in the garage below, had survived the day. The fire marshal wouldn't allow him to return, but he'd been told he had a new skylight over the master bedroom—in a location that had been a solid roof.

The sweet spot in the whole mess was that the party sounds had reached an intolerable level by mid-afternoon that day. His dog Emma had started whining and pacing nervously, so Adam had decided the two of them needed to leave for the day. They'd escaped the loud music and other sounds of revelry by visiting his parents in Kenai for the night. For that reason, they'd both survived. Now everything that hadn't been destroyed three weeks ago fit nicely into a single suitcase, the one he'd taken to his parents' place that day.

Owning a house signified roots. Putting down permanent roots where he'd found a job he loved—his first full-time teaching position after college—made sense. Knowing little about Anchorage and less about buying a house meant dependence on a real estate agent.

But enough was enough. He could only give a new agent a few weeks before he'd give up and rent. Living in someone's guest room hadn't been a joyful experience. Especially on weekends. And Emma didn't love living with her human grandparents in Kenai with only weekend visits from her owner. In another hour, he'd kneel down and wait for her to leap into his arms. That made the trip to Kenai, and the upcoming night in his mom and dad's less-than-private guest room, worth it.

He turned into Merrill Field Airport and soon pulled up next to his blue and white Cessna 172. He wasn't surprised to see that the tie-down space next to his had only a car in it, no airplane. His friend Austin often took off early for the weekend. Adam turned at the sound of an airplane coming in his direction and saw Austin's red and white Piper Super Cub moving down the taxiway. As Adam began his preflight inspection, Austin taxied into the tie-down spot and turned off the engine.

Austin hopped out of his plane. He shouted over the noise of a plane taking off, "I wondered about you when you weren't here earlier."

Adam grinned. "We do seem to be on the same flight schedule lately. My question for you is, why are you back so soon?"

"There's a storm coming, and I didn't want to get stuck in my cabin for days. I went out a day early to have a short weekend of sorts, but I have an important business meeting Monday morning." Austin began tying down his airplane with the rope connected to the ground, starting with the left wing.

"I can't believe that I haven't checked the weather report." Adam blew out a breath. Looking to the sky, he turned in a circle to visually see what was going on. "That's a beginner's mistake. I may have lost brain cells in this house hunt. Looking for a house isn't for wimps."

Austin chuckled. "No, it's not. My search took eight months two years ago. That's why I'm not moving anytime soon. But don't worry, my friend. The weather's supposed to be clear until tomorrow or Sunday. The storm's still out over the Pacific. Now, if you want to fly back tomorrow night, you may—or may not—have a problem."

"I don't *have* to be back by Monday. That's the beauty of a professor's life during the summer." Adam stared at the propeller in front of him. Should he stay on the ground this weekend? What would that look like? A hotel, no Emma, no family.

"Did you decide not to go?" Austin asked.

He turned toward his friend. "Huh?"

Austin had finished tying down the other wing and the tail. "You stood in one place so long that I thought you were changing your mind about going."

"No. I'm going. I can always rent a car and drive back if I need to."

"That is the good thing about a destination with road access."

Adam chuckled. "You wouldn't change the location of your cabin for anything."

"You're probably right." Austin grinned. "You'll need to fly out and visit when the salmon are running."

Adam's mouth watered at the prospect of fresh salmon. Nothing from a store or restaurant could compare to one he'd caught himself. "It's a deal."

Austin started toward his car. "Give Emma a doggie treat for me."

"My parents have been spoiling their 'granddog'—their substitute grandchild until one of their five sons *finally* gives them a human one. The emphasis is my mother's."

Austin laughed. "I miss being with my parents, but at times like these, I'm glad they're in Florida and visit once or twice a year."

"Mine have taken to technology as a means of scouting for wives for their sons. Mom joined an online dating service when the company had a free month and chose some likely candidates."

"And?" Austin asked as he unlocked the door and opened it.

"I politely told her I'd find my own wife, thank you very much."

"Did that stop her?"

Adam sighed. "It didn't even slow her down. The next day, she emailed over a couple more candidates."

Grinning, his friend got into his car and drove off, leaving Adam with his preflight inspection and his thoughts. He focused on ensuring the plane would stay airborne, checking each of the small details that could mean the difference between arriving safely in Kenai or making an emergency landing somewhere in between—never in a dense forest, he hoped.

With the prop spinning well by hand, tire and fuel levels correct, and the many other items on his inspection list checking out, he untied the ropes, climbed into the cockpit and continued his inspection there. With that done, he opened his window, shouted "Clear!" closed it, and started the engine. The prop flared to life. Now, he needed for his personal life to do the same.

Adam radioed for permission from the tower, taxied over the same path Austin had recently taken, then waited for departure clearance.

Given permission to use runway sixteen, he got up to speed and took off, quickly getting to the proper altitude and choosing the direct path to the Kenai airport, only a ten-minute drive from his parent's house. The highway from Anchorage to Kenai twisted along the shore to his left as he crossed the wide salt water of Turnagain Arm, really a bay. That drive took about two and a half hours because it followed the shoreline then crossed through a mountain pass. He understood that the powers that be had discussed a bridge years ago, but it had never been built, so his as-the-crow-flies flight trimmed off two hours. He loved being able to get somewhere quickly in Alaska. So often, the roads needed to use indirect routes because of mountains and water. His plane didn't.

Familiar wilderness passed under him with its winding rivers and dozens of lakes, including those on the Swan Lake Canoe Route, one of his favorite places in the world. Cabins, often only used on weekends and during warmer months, would be down there too.

About halfway to his destination, he took out his phone and called his dad. The invention of the cell phone made traveling in small planes much easier than his grandfather had described. The older man had made it sound as challenging as chiseling a message in stone and flinging it out the window to let someone know where he was.

Civilization began to appear with more roads and buildings as he neared the small city of Kenai. Adam called the tower, landed after receiving permission, then taxied over to the guest tie-down area.

His dad waited for him in a big, black pickup truck, with a little white dog's nose pressed against the passenger window. Grinning, Adam stepped out of the plane. His dad reached over and popped open the passenger door. Emma raced across the pavement and leaped into his arms.

"Did you miss me, girl?" He ruffled the fur at Emma's ears, something he knew she loved.

His dad stepped out and leaned against the truck's front end, resting his hands on the hood. "Did she miss you? She cried for an hour after you left last week."

Yet one more reason to find a place to live as soon as possible. Emma needed to be with her owner. Adam carried his dog over to the truck, not letting her down again without her leash. Now that she'd calmed down, she might actually notice a loud sound or distraction. "I miss my daily walks with her."

"Seen any decent housing options?" his dad asked as he pulled his door open again.

Adam opened the truck's front passenger-side door, climbed in, and settled Emma on his lap. "No. Not a one." He buckled up as his dad started the engine. "With the options Dennis showed me, I feel like giving up and renting next week."

"Maybe you should change real estate agents. I'm sure there are pretty ones out there."

Adam rolled his eyes. He'd never choose a business connection based on appearance. That sounded like a certain recipe for disaster. But Holly Harris fit the bill as a qualified agent. And she'd mesmerized him with her smile, dark hair, and sparkling brown eyes. He glanced over at his father. The last thing he'd do would be to mention her to his dad. The message would track right back to his mother. Both parents would check out her website to see if her bio met their standards for a future daughter-in-law.

Some children had one parent who wanted them married; he had two.

One thing he did know about Holly Harris was that she was a hard worker. When he'd given her feedback on a writing assignment, she'd applied it to the next one. He'd seen her skill level jump significantly during their two classes together. Holly would be a motivated real estate agent.

She was the one agent he wanted to call. Why shouldn't he? If something beyond business happened to come out of it, so much the better. He glanced at his father out of the corner of his eye, hoping he didn't appear so happy that his dad asked why. Holly Harris didn't wear a wedding ring. She appeared to be available. And she hadn't mentioned a significant other this morning when she'd said who would help her with the house. Would contacting her be a good idea or a huge mistake?

Chapter Three

Holly flopped onto her couch, curling up and facing its back. She settled into the cushions and some of the day's stress disappeared. Then the shoes she'd forgotten to remove called her back to reality. Letting her feet dangle off the edge of the couch, she felt her shoes slide off for the second time that day. Adrenaline rushed in as she remembered herself once again mid-Mount Everest-like porch scaling.

Sitting up, she rested her elbows on her knees, her chin in her palms. "Long, long Friday. Followed by another long day tomorrow. And possibly a third, if I can't squeeze the rest into Saturday." She tapped her forehead with her forefinger. "Focus, Holly, focus. One task at a time." Once she'd cleaned up the house, she knew it would sell. She just hoped a buyer appeared soon. Very soon.

A bird chirped outside, then the refrigerator came on. Small sounds she barely registered on a normal day boomed around her. The quiet in her house unsettled her. There were moments like these when she wished she hadn't agreed to let her girls travel Alaska with her parents. She still had weeks until her hectic, busy, child-filled life returned. She was counting the seconds.

Rolling onto her back, she lay still for a minute before sitting up again and staring blankly at the wall. Life felt . . . off. Standing, she rolled her shoulders and leaned over to stretch her back, considering her options for her evening. She needed to address dinner and de-stressing. Both could happen at the same time if she made a pie.

Stepping from the small living room into the even smaller kitchen required just a few steps. She opened the fridge and leaned on the door. Cheese, milk, leftover cooked broccoli— Bree had brought dinner the night before—and ham would make a delicious quiche. She'd hidden the ham in the corner of the fruit drawer the night before, hoping Bree didn't notice she'd accidentally bought the kind with nitrates in it. That would be worth a short lecture. Dr. Briana Harris loved her family, and wanted to be sure they knew the science behind everything.

A knock at the door made her glance up.

"It's Jemma," her sister called through the closed door. Holly shoved the ham back in the fruit drawer—in case Bree had come too- shut the fridge with her hip, and hustled over to the door.

Opening it, she found only Jemma with a cake-sized box in her arms. "Dessert. I thought you could use some chocolate about this time."

Holly reached for the box. "Thank you!"

"Real food first."

Holly glanced around the corner. "Is Bree coming too?" She hoped she'd hidden the ham well enough.

Her sister laughed. "No. But I guess she's been an influence on me since she moved nearby last year." Jemma handed Holly the box. "Forget what I said before. Eat this whenever you want."

Holly ushered her sister inside and closed the door. "Can you stay for dinner?"

Jemma nodded. "I'd love to. Nathaniel is at a corporate event and said I didn't need to go, for which I'm very thankful. I've attended hundreds of events, both large and small. When you're busy because you're the one in charge, they're okay. Without that, they range from tolerable to boring beyond words."

"Take a seat." Holly pointed at the chair closest to the kitchen. "I'll make quiche."

Her sister remained standing. "*Yum.* But are you sure you want to cook? I brought dessert to prevent you from getting into pie mode. Your description of that house made me think today had presented its challenges." Jemma got the concerned big sister expression on her face that Holly knew well.

"After all the junk I moved around today, I need to unwind. Pie is my unwind. Sweet, savory, it doesn't matter. But first . . ." She lifted the lid on the box. "Chocolate cheesecake?"

Jemma nodded.

"Forks." She pointed at her silverware drawer. "This will provide energy."

Chuckling, Jemma did as asked, handing one to Holly who immediately scooped up a bite of the dessert and slid it into her mouth.

"Oh, my. That's wonderful. I know better than to ask for the recipe though."

Jemma grinned, then dipped her own fork into the chocolate concoction and brought it to her mouth to taste. "This is a giant yum. You'll have to ask the bakery I stopped at in Anchorage for the recipe. I was in the big city today for an estate sale. That photo of the crime scene—a.k.a. the house you're listing—told me you'd need something sweet tonight."

"Good decision," Holly said around another mouthful of chocolate heaven. Closing the lid on temptation, she put the sealed box in her fridge. Out of sight. But not out of mind. "I'll be back for you," she said before she started to close the door. Stopping herself, she rescued the ham from its banishment and set it next to her other supplies on the counter.

Jemma positioned herself on the chair Holly had pointed to earlier. "Watching you make a pie crust always amazes me. Where did your baking gene come from?"

"Remember when Mom broke her leg?"

"I do, but I was away in college, so I didn't see her until she'd had the cast replaced with a walking boot."

"Well, Grandma Harris spent a month at our house helping Mom. I was finishing high school and woefully unprepared for the world as far as Grandma was concerned. She took it upon herself to teach me to make a pie one afternoon after school. I liked doing it, so we made a pie every day, and started giving them to neighbors. They'd finish it off and bring back the pan for another."

"If Mom's mother had been available, the story would be different."

Holly measured the flour for the crust into the food processor. "She'd have shown me how to order takeout with style."

"She taught me everything she knew one summer."

Plopping in the rest of the crust's ingredients, Holly repeatedly hit the pulse button on the processor, waiting until it looked right. "You're a pro, so she was a fine instructor."

"So true. I can order with the best of them."

"And you toast a fine bagel—topped with cream cheese and jam, of course."

In her quiet time, something that she had more of now that her twins weren't babies anymore, Holly continued on her quest for the perfect crust. She knew she'd come close a time or two. After emptying the mixture onto a floured spot on her kitchen island, she gathered it together, took her rolling pin out of a cupboard, and went to work. Tension eased away every time she did this.

As she rolled the dough into a round, the room disappeared, leaving just her and the crust. She gently lifted it onto the glass pie plate and settled it into the bottom before forming the edge. Releasing a deep breath, she felt the rest of the day's troubles fall away. Jemma spoke when she reached for a bowl to mix up the filling.

"It's fun to see your stress vanish. I always feel better when I watch you make a pie." She held up her hand. "Not enough to try baking one myself, so don't worry."

Holly melodramatically put her right hand on her chest. "Thank you! For a moment, my life flashed in front of my eyes. Jemma. Kitchen. Not compatible." She quickly combined the ingredients for the cheesy mixture, poured it into the crust, and slid her finished product into the oven.

"I'm sorry none of us could help today. Were you able to accomplish much?"

Holly grinned at her. "You're really asking if the photo still matches the scene? The answer is a resounding yes!"

"Not that I'm not here for you, sis, but that's too bad. I thought it might be less of a mess in another part of the house."

"No. I did some of the easy work." Holly pictured the bags of clothes and toys she'd hauled to the second-hand store earlier. "Well, not all easy, but doable. On the flip side, the owners said I could keep whatever I wanted, so I brought home a couple of toys that I think the girls will like."

"Heard from Mom and Dad today?"

"I receive photos every few hours when they're within cell phone reception. Sometimes that's a dozen in a day. Once they didn't send any for two days, and I started to panic. Then Dad called and put the girls on the phone. They'd gone up the Fortymile River with Michael's brother, spent the day with him, then overnighted in the campground where Bree did last year."

"Only in their RV, not a tent."

Holly chuckled. "I'm sure Bree would have preferred that."

"She still talks about that tent. Abbie and Ivy are old enough that they'll remember this summer's trip with their grandparents."

"I know. I love that. I just wish I could have taken time off and gone with them." Holly pointed to her phone. "Check out the cute one of them with the stuffed moose in Tok. I always loved going there when I was a kid."

Jemma picked up the phone and flipped through the pictures. "Adorable as always. I'm excited to have one of my own."

The spoon she'd been rinsing off clanked into the stainless steel sink. "Are you . . ."

Her sister's eyes widened. "No! Absolutely not." She paused. "At least, I don't think so."

"Nathaniel won't be like Grant, my former husband. He'll be thrilled when you do get that news."

Jemma fingered her hair in an uneasy way. "Being a mother scares me more than a little bit. I don't know if I'm ready for it. Talk about responsibility!"

"If I can be a mom, so can you."

Jemma fidgeted. "I do know Nathaniel will be with me through the process. He may be a bit nervous about fatherhood after his own crazy childhood, but now that he and his dad have patched things up, he's more comfortable with the idea."

"Their guys-only fishing trip in Mexico last winter was a good idea."

"I missed him, but he needed to heal more. They both did." Jemma grinned. "Nathaniel still talks about the fish that got away."

Laughing, Holly washed her hands. Then she returned to the couch where her evening had begun, and Jemma sat beside her. "I'm glad you stopped by. I wish Bree could have come too."

"Just be grateful she doesn't have to work Saturday so she can help."

Holly sighed. "I wish she and Michael lived out in the Matanuska-Susitna Valley near us. I'd love that after they get married. But . . ."

"They both enjoy city living, so being out here in the Valley in small-town Palmer or Wasilla wouldn't be right for them. At least they'll be nearby when Bree starts having babies. Our kids will grow up together. I love that idea."

That made twice in a half hour that Jemma had mentioned future parenthood. This from a sister who clearly adored her nieces, but had never before talked about having kids.

Before leaving, Jemma had taken their plates into the kitchen, washed them up, and put away the leftovers. The luxury of a dishwasher sat near the top of Holly's wish list for her next home, that and a full-sized washer and dryer. The compact one in the hall closet worked well right now, but the girls' clothes would get larger and larger. She dreaded the days of teen-sized clothing and twenty loads a week.

Maybe her dreams would come true before then. She prayed they would. Her success meant a larger washer and a *dishwasher.*

Silence reigned in her house. By this time in the day, that was the norm, since her five-year-olds had an early bedtime. Holly's bed called, begging her to come join it early and rest for what would surely be a long day tomorrow. Her laptop said otherwise.

She heeded her laptop's call, bringing it over to her makeshift desk—a stool pulled up to the kitchen counter. With the computer powered up, she opened her writing software and read through the previous night's effort. Her characters Rose and Collin knew each other. Now, they'd need to work together to solve the puzzle they'd stumbled upon. A mystery combined with romance. She leaned her elbows on the counter and smiled. *Let the games begin.*

She typed a sentence, paused to read through it, decided it was garbage, and deleted it. She typed another sentence, paused a few seconds longer, then did the same thing. Running her fingers through her hair, she stared at the flashing cursor on the screen. Words usually joyfully flowed from her brain to her fingers to her computer. Now, zip. Time and quiet, her usual formula for success, had met. So what had happened?

She hadn't had a problem like this since . . . "No! Not again!" Dr. O'Connell had happened.

Holly jumped to her feet and stomped across the room. Every time he'd returned one of her papers, she'd taken it to her car and driven to the nearby hospital's parking lot so she could cry where other students wouldn't see her. Every single time. She'd turn in her best work, and he'd pick it apart.

When she'd thought the horror had stopped with the end of the semester, she'd walked into her next required English course and found him standing at the front of the room. The listed professor had moved away suddenly when his wife got a job in Paris, so Dr. O'Connell had taken over for him. Understandable, but nearly intolerable.

Finally, she'd asked family and friends to read a short story she'd written for the class. They'd raved over it, so she'd breathed a sigh of relief. She could write. So, if she wasn't the problem, it had to be her nitpicking professor who just didn't like her work.

She'd begun watching every word she wrote, making the writing process time-consuming and painful. But by the end of the semester, she had started to let go of his criticism. She had a style of her own, and she'd rolled with it. Until now.

Staring out the window at the empty street, she counted to ten. "I won't let you do this to me again. Collin and Rose *will* fall in love. They *will* solve this mystery." With a single nod, she returned to her computer and wrote a paragraph without stopping to evaluate it. Then she pushed on and wrote a page. Grinning, she kept going. "Dr. Difficult, I win. And I hope we never meet again."

Adam pulled a computer tablet out of his bag, a convenient way to check in with his work on the go. And he always seemed to be on the move from one guest room to another. While he searched for a place to sit, Emma chose the one comfortable piece of furniture in the room—the bed—and put her head on his pillow.

Adam perched on the edge of the singularly most uncomfortable chair he'd ever known in his life—a pink rose-upholstered, wood-framed, white-painted, barely padded, and thoroughly hideous piece of furniture—and brought up his university email account. He then explained to a student from the previous semester why he had indeed earned his poor grade, that As and Bs were reserved for those who turned in all their assignments, and he fielded a few questions from others about upcoming fall classes.

Drumming the edge of the tablet, he debated working on his personal project. He heard his mother making cooking sounds in the kitchen. His dad flipped on the TV.

Adam set the computer to the side and picked up Emma, stretching out on his bed with her on his chest—her favorite place to sleep. The twin bed was a little short, but the only thing that came close to comfortable in the room. The headboard reminded him of the one he'd had during his childhood in Alaska's capital, Juneau. The dresser beside the door might also have been the one he'd stared at across the room from his bed all those years. But back then, both had a natural light oak stain. Now they'd been painted a creamy

27

white with parts of the finish rubbed off, making it appear worn and old. Mom called her design plan shabby chic. He didn't see the "chic" in it.

When his dad retired from teaching high school math, his parents moved to Kenai, a place his father had said was "a small town he could drive out of if he wanted to." Apparently, living in Juneau with only air and water connections to the rest of the world had bothered the man the entire twenty-two years the family had lived there. No more. His parents moved in five years ago, bought a motor home within a month, and drove it that summer from Kenai all the way to Seattle, Washington. Adam suspected it was to prove the point that doing so was possible and that his father could drive out anytime he felt the need.

When Adam heard the rising sounds of music on what sounded like one of his dad's action or adventure movies, he knew that quiet wouldn't be available for a couple of hours. Emma jumped down and whimpered at the door at the same time he caught a whiff of popcorn—probably what his mother had been making in the kitchen. Adam got to his feet and opened the door, the popcorn smell filling the room. Emma raced ahead of him. When humans had popcorn, she knew she'd have a special doggy treat, since buttered and salted popcorn wasn't the best thing for canines.

When he entered the living room, his mother jumped in with her opinions on his house hunt. Speaking over the volume of the TV, she said, "Adam, I called a few friends, and one has a niece in Anchorage who is a real estate agent."

"An unmarried niece?"

His father paused the movie, probably to enjoy the scene playing out in front of him.

"Why, yes." His mother placed her hand over her chest in an innocent manner that would have made Scarlett O'Hara proud. "Why do you ask?" After a second dramatic pause, she added, "She sounds like a lovely young woman, and you would be her first client."

This hit a new low. A blind date with a brand-new real estate agent. His waffling about Holly ended. "I spoke to one of my former students today—a woman who earned her degree, but chose to become a real estate agent after graduation." He *had* spoken to her. He hadn't lied. "I'll check with her in the morning, but I'm hoping to fly back to see some properties tomorrow afternoon."

His dad shook his head. "That's a lot of flying back and forth, son." Always frugal, he added, "Fuel costs add up."

"I know. But it's the only way I can see to make this all work out. I need a house, and you can't buy what you haven't seen. At least I couldn't." Now, he just had to hope Holly could make this happen, or his parents might make him feel obligated to contact the "niece." He needed to win this one.

Chapter Four

Cell phone in hand, Holly plopped down onto the chair she and her sisters had dragged back onto the porch. She still wasn't sure where she'd gotten the energy yesterday to drag it across the porch, down the step, across a stretch of lawn to the side of the porch, then onto the trunk she'd also carried there. Jemma and Bree occupied a matching bench placed beside her chair, the only other piece of furniture on the porch.

Jemma leaned forward to pull sandwiches out of the large bag of takeout she'd set on the porch floor. As she took out the first one out, she read, "chicken salad," and set it on her lap. "Avocado, tomato, and cheese." She handed the wrapped sandwich to Bree. "I didn't even hear you place your order, but I know this one must belong to you. It sounds very healthy." Holding up another sandwich, she said, "The last one's unmarked."

Holly reached over for the sandwich. "It's mine."

Jemma moved it out of her reach. "What if it's a mistake? How do you know it's yours?"

Holly shrugged. "I tell them to give me whatever the special is."

Jemma handed it to her. "What if you don't like the special?"

Unwrapping the paper around her food, Holly said, "First, everything they make is tasty. Second, I'm a working, single mom of active, five-year-old twin girls. I eat when I can and whatever is available."

Bree shook her head. "You need to think of yourself sometimes." She pointed her thumb at the house behind her. "This place is a perfect example. I still can't believe you told them you'd clean it up."

Holly unwrapped her sandwich. Layers of meat—ham, roast beef, and what must be turkey—along with two types of cheese greeted her. A meat lover's special sandwich wasn't her favorite. Maybe she did need to ask for what she wanted.

Chewing, Holly tapped her phone's screen to take it to email. After swallowing, she said, "Well, I knew it was the means to getting the listing. I wanted their decision to be so easy that they saw it as a no-brainer." After checking two messages from other agents about new listings, she opened the next message, one from a couple who'd been her clients for months. She stared at the email on the small screen.

"No!"

Jemma leaned over. "What?"

Holly handed the device to her sister and slouched into the hard seat, barely able to process what she'd just read. "This can't be happening. People don't realize that a real estate agent isn't paid until the day the deal closes. You can show a couple eighty-nine houses in Anchorage and the

Mat-Su Valley, use many tanks of gas, even take them to lunch every once and a while. Then they can decide to rent, and you get nothing!"

Bree set her sandwich on her lap. "Harv and Anna? You spent so much time with that couple that we all met them. Jemma had them over for a barbecue at her house. They were starting to feel like family." Bree stood and came over to Holly, reaching down for a hug. "Maybe they'll be ready to buy in a few months."

Jemma answered before Holly could. "This says they leased a house for a year."

Holly groaned. "I *knew* they'd buy. I was counting on that sale." The twins would be in kindergarten this year and they needed school clothes. New studded tires were a must before the first snowfall. Not to mention heat this winter. Her house might be small, but it was older, so not well insulated. She needed sales *now*.

Bree and Jemma glanced at each other, then Bree nodded before turning to face Holly again.

"Michael and I could help you out if money's tight. We knew things had been slow for you lately and discussed this."

Holly glared at her.

"We'd be happy to do it. Being a single mom can be a challenge."

A sense of failure began to wash over Holly, but she pushed it away. "We'll be okay if I can close on a house in the next month or so."

When her sisters glanced at each other again, Holly stood. "Stop that! I'm fine. Ivy and Abbie are fine. I need a new client who will buy a house quickly. Problem solved."

"That's all, huh?"

"Yep." Her phone rang, and an unknown number showed on the screen. "Maybe this is the client I've been waiting for." She tapped the phone. "Hello?"

"Holly, this is Dr. O'Connell. Adam."

She felt her jaw drop.

"As it turns out, I need a real estate agent. Are you available?"

She worked her jaw as she tried to speak, struggling to squeeze out words. "Um, yes, sir. I am available."

"Could you show me some houses in the next few days?"

The mountain of stuff she and her sisters had hauled out of the house sat piled in the front yard, some awaiting a consignment store Jemma often bought from for her furniture rehabbing business, the rest ready for a junk hauler they'd called. The house needed to be scrubbed from top to bottom. If she worked into the night, she might finish up today and make the listing public tomorrow.

"I need to buy something as soon as possible."

Dollar signs danced in front of her eyes. "Sure! We can begin today." She dove into her usual process. "I'd like to show you a couple of properties—we'll call them sample homes—so you can tell me what you like and don't like about them. I've found that our search will go much better if I do that first."

"That sounds like an excellent idea. I'll be in Anchorage in an hour and drive straight to Palmer. When can I meet you at the real estate office?"

She'd lose time if she did that. Besides, once a potential buyer had seen you hanging off a roof, the need to set a proper business image became less of an issue. "I'm at that same house where you saw me yesterday. Let's leave from here."

"Excellent. I'll see you soon."

The call ended, and Holly stared at the phone. Was it a good thing she had a customer, or would spending time with Dr. O'Connell prove to be a bad thing? Maybe even a very bad thing? She hadn't enjoyed the hours she'd spent with him before.

Jemma wadded up her now empty sandwich wrapper. "I'm guessing that call brought you a new customer."

Holly nodded. "A former professor."

"Wow, it's great that she'd call you." Bree collected their trash and dropped it in the bag the food had come in.

"It's a he. Dr. O'Connell, my creative writing professor."

"Dr. Difficult?" Jemma asked.

"One and the same."

Bree glanced from one sister to the other. "Who?"

"He picked apart everything I wrote for his classes. There were moments when it got so bad that I thought I should drop my dream of writing novels."

"I missed so much when I was doing my residency in Boston and you two were here." Bree pointed at the partially untouched sandwich on Holly's lap. "The doctor says to eat."

Taking a bite of her lunch, she thought about her new customer. A minute later, she spoke. "I'll leave from here with Dr. O'Connell, but I'll need to have one of you stay here to greet the consignment guy."

Jemma raised her hand. "I can do it."

"I don't want to take you away from your business. Don't you have horrible furniture you need to turn into something new and awesome?"

Jemma gave a crooked smile. "Well, I have seen a few pieces here that I thought I'd have José drop off at my house.

I'll pay the owners the same amount they would have gotten from the store."

Holly waved her comment away. "They told me to dispose of everything. I'll send them a text to verify it's okay if you want, but you deserve to be paid for your work today. I doubt anything in here would have sold for enough to get a professional team in here to hold a sale."

Jemma laughed. "Hardly. My choices aren't standouts right now. You won't recognize them when I'm done."

Bree leaned back on the bench, one that was obviously more body friendly than the metal seat Holly sat on. "That's certainly true! She changed an ugly end table that came with Michael's condo—and I do mean *ugly*—into a padded ottoman I love. About your new customer, maybe he's a nice guy when he isn't teaching."

Jemma nodded. "I wondered the same thing."

Holly grinned. "One day I stopped to ask him a question as everyone left the class. Just the two of us were left in the room when he answered, so I can assume his true personality shone through. He oozed boring." The smiling man from yesterday morning had seemed different, though. "Today, he had more personality."

"On the phone?"

"No. I figured the two of you might think I'd made an error in judgment, so I thought it best not to tell you. But I'd better, since he could mention it." She explained the missing key, then patted the chair's arm. "This was moved because I used it to boost myself to the window sill."

Bree turned to the window. "Isn't the sill too high?"

Trust the scientifically-trained sister to see the hole in her explanation. "I lifted this chair onto a wooden trunk. I stepped onto the edge of the trunk, then the chair, and finally the window sill."

Both sisters stared at her, mouths open.

Jemma found her voice first. "You risked life and limb to get into this place?"

"It was either that or call a locksmith, and the charges for a professional would have come out of my pocket. Besides, the owners would have had to find a place to send me signed permission to hand to that locksmith. Unless a bear or moose out there had access to a fax machine, that wasn't happening."

Bree asked, "So your plan worked?"

"Almost. The chair slipped away as I stepped onto the sill. I had to grab for the roof."

"I see." Bree nodded slowly. "This man rescued you?"

"No. While I was dangling from the roof . . ."

Both sisters winced.

"Dr. O'Connell walked up. He said he was living nearby, and thought I was breaking into the house."

Bree wagged her finger at her. "So that's why he knew to call *you*."

Jemma nudged Bree with her elbow. "Maybe he's interested in Holly for more than a new house."

Holly shuddered. "No, thank you. Matt's nice and stable. I know he will be a good father to my girls."

"I guess that means you've let him meet the girls."

"Um, I'm planning on doing that soon."

Jemma rolled her eyes. "A man you've been dating for months—"

"Casually dating."

"*Casually* dating for months hasn't met the most important people in your life? Two lively, adorable girls."

Holly cleared her throat. "There hasn't been a right time to do that."

Jemma made an ugly sigh. "At least he knows they exist."

Holly forced a smile. "He will this weekend."

Her big sister glared at her. "We talked about this months ago. You still haven't told him?"

She knew Jemma was right, but how did you tell a man you had kids? Did you do it early on, when he might reject you because of them, or wait until you knew him better and hope he cared enough to stick around?

Bree asked, "Do you think he's going to be happier about it if you wait longer?"

"I want to make sure there's a possibility for a future for us before I let him meet them."

Bree rested her elbows on her thighs, her chin on her thumbs. "Meeting and telling are very different."

Holly considered her words. Had she made a mistake? A man might be more than a little startled when he learned a woman had not only one but two kids. "You're right. I'll tell him the next time we're on a date. I hope we're getting closer to a permanent relationship."

"Whoa! I didn't realize you were in love with the handsome trooper."

Holly fought the sadness that sunk through her when she thought about love. "I don't know if I know what love is. It may not be possible."

Bree said, "Sure it is. Look at Michael and me. And Jemma and Nathaniel."

Holly blew out a breath. "Neither of you had a husband leave you."

Jemma shook her head. "More than five years later, I still

feel shocked whenever I think about what he did to you. Who leaves a pregnant wife?" Her sister stood and picked up a pile of books she'd set on the porch.

Bree said, "Not just pregnant, but pregnant with twins. I wish we'd been living near you when all that happened."

"Me too." Holly set her lunch down. "I was a twenty-year-old college student a thousand miles from home. I don't know how I did it, but I finished up the semester. Then I packed up what I wanted to keep and went home to Mom and Dad."

She stood and tossed the remainder of her sandwich into the paper bag. "Grant told me before we got married that he didn't want kids."

Jemma leaned against a front porch post, books in hand. "He just didn't mention he'd leave if you accidentally got pregnant."

"No. But he didn't leave the day I told him I was pregnant. A month later I had an ultrasound, and they found twins." The memory had dulled over time but still stung. Avoiding it, Holly studied the porch. Focus on work. That had always gotten her through. The paint wasn't peeling, just dirty. A good wash with the hose should do for this area.

"Then he left?" Bree asked.

Unfortunately, her sisters weren't ready to drop it. "Dropped me off at home. Returned an hour later to get his things. Divorce papers arrived soon after. At least he gave me full custody of the girls."

Jemma carried the books over to the consignment pile on the lawn. Returning, she said, "I've heard of some messy divorces, friends who had to fight for everything, so we'll consider it his loss and our gain. I love being an auntie to those girls."

"Me too." Bree got to her feet. "Ready to clean?"

"Never." Holly grinned. "I want this house on the market though. I'll need to change clothes in about an hour."

"You brought business clothes?" Bree asked as she walked through the door with Jemma on her heels.

"I learned years ago to always have a change of clothes in the trunk, something that packs easily. With two babies . . ."

"Explain no more. I haven't done that in my medical practice, but from now on, I'll remember to have a spare set ready. Kids can be hard on a pediatrician's clothing."

"I don't even want to know," Jemma said from the kitchen. "I don't have children yet and don't want to fear the little things."

Bree stopped with a closet door halfway open. "But you aren't . . ."

"No. Definitely not. But I hope someday to have kids."

"Me too." Bree giggled in a way that had both Holly and Jemma watching her. She pulled a vacuum out of a closet, plugged it in, and turned it on. They watched her for a second, then both went back to work. She'd bet a dozen donuts, something she didn't do lightly, that Bree had a secret. She just hoped it wasn't a baby secret since she and Michael hadn't yet walked down the aisle. That would complicate her life in so many ways.

Chapter Five

The sisters worked in quiet harmony together, so much so that Holly didn't notice the passage of time. When she checked her phone, her heart started racing. Close to an hour had passed. She hurried over to the kitchen island, dropped the window cleaner and paper towel, then hustled outside for her duffel bag.

With the trunk open in front of her, she glanced down at the grimy present state of her lower half then pawed through the goods in the bag pulling out a top, pants, and dressier shoes—anything would be nicer than her formerly white, now tan, sneakers.

When she stepped inside the house, Bree said, "I hope you have clean things from top to bottom. You've really gotten into this project, and it's gotten on you."

Holly grinned. "Very funny." She hustled over to the powder room and stripped off her dirty clothing. Pulling a simple, black, long-sleeved top over her head then slipping into black trousers and flat shoes left her looking a bit goth.

40

After gathering up her dirty clothes, she raced to her car and found a colorful scarf in the bag.

If only she could improve her love life as easily as she changed from a grimy house cleaner into a business professional. Maybe it should be colorful and not boring, like her clothing. Not that Matt was boring. He felt steady and solid. If their times together didn't have a sense of excitement to them, as she'd like, it might be her problem.

She'd yet to fall for a man beyond her first husband. And when she looked back at that relationship with mature eyes, she often wondered if her heart had been filled with nothing more than admiration for a man who seemed to have it all together at an age when so few did. He hadn't, of course, because he'd left her in the end.

Back inside the house, Holly did a walk-through of both levels of the house, making notes as she went. Clipboard in hand, she found her sisters back on the front porch, sitting on the bench.

Jemma stretched out her legs. "We're taking a break."

Bree stretched out beside her. "I think we're almost done. You can probably make the listing live tomorrow."

Holly leaned against the door frame. "I'll be in excellent shape financially if I can sell a house to Dr. O'Connell and sell this place too." Straightening, she turned back to the open living area. "Maybe he'll buy this house, and I can close quickly."

"What does he want?"

"He didn't say, but I'd guess something simple, and easy."

Jemma grinned. "Boring."

"Yeah. I guess that's what I'm thinking. There isn't a thing wrong with this house. In fact, it may be someone's dream house. But I'd personally prefer something more unusual, maybe with high ceilings and beams. Or stairs elegantly curving upward." Holly blew out a deep breath. "But I'll *always* be grateful for the two-bedroom cottage that Great-aunt Grace left me here in Palmer." She pulled out her phone and checked the clock. "He could be here any time now."

She looked up as a motorcycle turned down the previously quiet street. A man in a black leather jacket rode up, pulled into the driveway, turned off the engine, and climbed off the motorcycle. Holly wondered if the homeowners had told someone the house was on the market. When he pulled off his helmet, then turned her way, her mouth dropped.

"Can *I* be a real estate agent?" Jemma asked from her left side, apparently not content to sit and watch.

Bree spoke from her other side, reaching around Holly to nudge Jemma. "That's no way to talk. You're married."

"Married, but I can see. I wonder who he is."

Holly realized her mouth was still open. Closing it, she stared. "Dr. Difficult."

Her sisters wheeled around to her. "*That's* Dr. Difficult?!"

Bree said, "We're getting you an eye exam appointment ASAP. For that matter, I might have to get out my stethoscope and give you a physical now. Something must be wrong. This isn't the man you described."

Dr. O'Connell walked toward them, each step oozing a male force she hadn't known he possessed. Dr. Difficult had vanished to be replaced with an unexpected . . . more. Those over-the-top sexy men in ads for cologne could take lessons from him.

Jemma shook her head. As he neared them, she whispered, "And the twinkle in his blue eyes when he smiles—what's wrong with you? You didn't mention that all the girls were drooling over him."

"They weren't. That"—she nudged her elbow toward him—"isn't what he looked like in class. He was handsome, but not like this, more in an ordinary sort of way. *This* isn't the man I knew."

"Good thing, too," Jemma added. "They'd have knocked each other down as they tried to sit in the front row so they could be close to him."

"Shhh." Holly put her finger over her mouth. "Professional. I'm a real estate professional," she muttered, mostly to herself.

"Dr. Di—uh, O'Connell."

Both sisters put their hands over their mouths to stifle laughter.

"We aren't teacher and student anymore. Please call me Adam."

Holly winced. She couldn't call any professor by his or her first name, especially not him. His voice held memories of classes she'd struggled through. Remembering that, his appeal dropped down to normal. He was just a man searching for a house, her means of taking care of her family.

"I'm looking forward to helping you in your search. Let me introduce my sisters. Bree," she pointed to her, "and Jemma. Now, let's begin with the things you like about what you see outside." She motioned to the yard and the neighborhood beyond that.

"Other than the fact that I'm outside and enjoy the outdoors? Nothing."

"Okaaay." This might be more challenging than she'd expected. "Maybe I should flip the question. What don't you like?"

"The yard is small. The houses are all similar and too close together."

"I understand. Maybe the interior will give additional clues to your needs." Holly moved toward the front door and through it with Dr. O'Connell behind her. Bree and Jemma stepped around them and headed toward the kitchen—the room that still needed the most attention.

"Same questions," Holly said. "Likes and dislikes. Details will be useful."

Scanning the open living area from left to right, he said, "High ceilings, open from the kitchen to the rest of the living area. It's just . . . uninteresting."

Stepping forward, she said, "I'm beginning to understand. Let's go upstairs." He followed her to the upstairs landing. Never comfortable touring the master bedroom with a single man, she said, "I'll stay in the doorway of each room as you walk around it. Everything you tell me will help me with your search. Please don't be shy."

He chuckled. "I've never been accused of being shy." Walking from the entrance to the window across the room he glanced around. At the window, he pushed the curtains to the side and frowned. Making a mental note that the man didn't want to live in a subdivision, she watched him disappear into the master bathroom. He stepped back into the room. "This bedroom and bath are fine. Just not in the—"

"Right location."

Dr. O'Connell gave a slow grin. "Exactly. You're good at this. I don't want a slice of suburbia."

"The other bedrooms and the hall bath that serves them are a standard size. If you give me a few minutes to check on something, we can go to the next home."

He nodded, then wandered out the door and down the hall.

Holly rushed downstairs. She knew the next house she'd set up in another subdivision would not appeal to him. One she'd shown a couple of weeks ago in Wasilla came to mind. He might like that *if* she could schedule it with a half hour's notice. At the kitchen island, she pulled her computer tablet out of the tote bag she'd left by the door.

"Is he being a Dr. Difficult?" Jemma whispered as she watched the stairs.

"No. He just doesn't like typical subdivision houses." She found the house and dialed the listing agent. At the agent's reply, Holly rocked back on her heels. The owners required twenty-four hours' notice for a viewing, so she couldn't show him that house today. After she'd ended the call with the promise to call back after speaking with her customer, her panic level flew up another notch. She heard Dr. O'Connell's deep voice from upstairs, so he was either having a conversation with himself or on his phone. She opted for the latter.

Bree set down the bottle of spray cleaner, a natural variety she'd brought along with some other natural cleaners, and asked in a low voice, "What's going on?"

Holly pointed up the stairs. "He doesn't want a house like this one, *or* the next one I've booked."

"Oh, so he might think you don't understand if you take him there? Tell him this is it for today."

"I can't do that. If there's one thing I learned as his student, it's that he expects to have promises met. I said I'd show him two houses so I could gauge his needs. I *have* to show him two houses."

Jemma bit her lip. "Hmm. Is it a requirement that the second house be for sale, or did you just tell him he'd look at two houses?"

"I said it was just to look at them."

"Show him our house. It isn't too far away, it's on acreage, and other than four outside walls, it doesn't have much in common with this house."

Holly let the idea sink in. "Why not?" She pulled her sister into a hug. "Thank you."

"You can even show him my business headquarters across the street if you think he might prefer an older house. Ignore the craft and sewing explosion in the dining room."

"You're the best!"

"Hey, what about me?" Bree asked. "I can offer our, rather Michael's, condo in Anchorage if you need it."

Holly grinned. "Thanks, Bree. You're both the best."

Jemma glanced up the stairs. Dr. O'Connell was still on the phone. "I'll run home and make sure everything is ready." Her sister picked up her purse and hurried out the door. "Don't worry. I'll come back and help you afterward."

A minute later, Holly watched Dr. O'Connell come down the stairs. Handsome he might be, but it would take more than nice hair and a killer smile to make her forget the two semesters she'd spent as his student. She'd never worked so hard for so little praise in her life. Sure, she'd received As in both classes, but she'd earned them and then some.

"Dr. O'Connell, I've scheduled our next house. We can drive in my car." They walked toward the door.

"Adam, please."

She just smiled. "This is my car." Holly pointed to the slightly beat-up, but clean, small, silver car. "The next house is quite different. As I said earlier, I'm simply scoping out your wants and needs right now."

"I'm game. Is it in the Valley too?"

"Yes, in Palmer." She unlocked his door then went around to the other side to open hers. "We can discuss your specific needs when we've seen this next house. I know it might seem counterintuitive to view houses without knowing how many bedrooms and bathrooms you want, but I've learned that this is a better way and saves time in the end."

"Lead on, MacDuff."

Holly rolled her eyes.

"Not a Shakespeare fan?"

She hesitated a moment before deciding to speak openly. "Actually, I am. It always bothers me when his words are misquoted."

"Ouch. 'Lay on, MacDuff' sounds odd to modern ears." He gave her a look that said she might have impressed him. "I'll have to stay on my toes. Since you're a purist, I'll also mention that I don't expect this house hunt to be a battle to the death."

She chuckled. Verbal sparring with Dr. O'Connell intrigued her. She'd always thought him handsome, but difficult. Today, he'd become more real—and she liked the man more for it. At least the house hunt wouldn't be boring.

Chapter Six

They each got in and buckled up. Then Holly started on the short drive to Jemma's house. She'd been relieved at the suggestion of using this house with its contemporary wall of windows and gorgeous view. Now though—she glanced at her passenger—she wondered if taking a customer to a relative's house would appear unprofessional.

Being one of Dr. O'Connell's students had taught her more than creative writing. This professor had demanded perfection, had insisted she push herself beyond what she'd done for the last assignment. The experience had exhausted her. She'd gleefully signed up for her next class with another professor and come close to having a meltdown when that hadn't gone as planned.

Now she sat behind the wheel of her car with Dr. O'Connell in the passenger seat. In some ways, their roles had reversed. But in others, they'd stayed pretty much the same. He was still in charge. A piece of her future hinged on whether or not she could make him happy.

She flipped on the turn signal to go down the road Jemma lived on, and they soon pulled into her driveway. When Dr. O'Connell reached for the door handle, she put her hand on his arm. "There's something I should tell you before we get out."

Jemma opened the front door and stood there waiting for them.

"Is that—?"

"Yes, that's my sister." Holly pointed toward the porch. "I had another house scheduled, but I could tell it wouldn't help. Jemma volunteered hers."

He shrugged, the simple gesture making him look more like a regular guy and less professorish. "I think it's a great idea. I like what I see so far. You're sure it isn't for sale?"

Holly laughed. "Absolutely positive. Jemma's husband Nathaniel had it custom built. Her house was across the street." Holly pointed.

"Wow, the man and woman lived across the street from each other and fell in love over time as they got to know each other. I thought that only happened in movies."

Holly laughed. "That wasn't quite their story. Other than being neighbors, of course." She popped open her car door. "Let's go see."

After stepping out of the car, Adam closed his eyes and took a deep breath, letting it out with a smile on his face. The man definitely wanted a sense of nature and space at home. A huge clue, but one that would narrow the search unless he was willing to drive farther to work every day.

As they neared the front steps, Jemma said, "Come in. I have coffee and cookies. We'll stay out of your way if you'd like to have a moment to talk over your house hunt."

Holly and Adam entered the house, her warily. She knew that in her and Nathaniel's early days of marriage, Jemma had tried to be her definition of a "good wife." Even though she didn't love cleaning, the bathrooms had sparkled, and she'd had dishpan hands. Jemma had also cooked a meal that Nathaniel felt compelled to eat. The cleaning was out of character but caused no problems—other than false expectations of the future. The food had sent Nathaniel to the emergency room that night.

"Get that look off your face, Holly. Nathaniel made both."

Dr. O'Connell glanced from one sister to the other, then grinned. His grin was *almost* enough to tempt her away from her kind, but oh-so-noncommittal, law enforcement officer. Did the professor have a wife or girlfriend tucked away somewhere? His eyes sparkled as he asked, "Is cooking not Jemma's specialty?"

A male voice from behind them said, "In our six months of marriage, I've discovered many things about my wife."

They all turned to watch Nathaniel as he came down the stairs.

"Not only is she stunningly gorgeous, but she's also a driven, successful entrepreneur."

Jemma lit up at his words.

Now at the bottom of the stairs, Jemma's husband stepped over to them. Laughing, he added, "She can also turn a dresser into fifteen different new things. But she should never, ever cook. The ER isn't somewhere I want to be again." He kissed Jemma on the cheek, then held his hand out to Dr. O'Connell. "Nathaniel Montgomery." They shook hands.

"You have a home I'd be happy to call my own."

"I spent months looking for the right building site and working with the architect." He turned toward the wall of windows that revealed a forest beyond. "Little did I know that the perfect building site would eventually bring me a wife. After some kicking and screaming." He laughed again. "Jemma, let's take Chloe for a walk so they can feel free to talk about our house."

"Excellent idea. She'll be thrilled to have an extra chance today to sniff everything on the street." Jemma pulled a leash off a hook by the front door, and she and Nathaniel left by a side door Holly knew led to the garage.

When the door snicked shut, Dr. O'Connell said, "I like almost everything I see. You chose well. You understand in a way that my first real estate agent never did."

"You had a different agent?" At his nod, she continued, "Did you sign an agreement to be exclusive to him or her? I can't work with you if you did." Holly watched the dollar signs fluttering up and out the tall windows.

"Definitely not."

She breathed a sigh of relief, then pulled her phone out of her purse to take notes. "Let's take a tour of the house. Again, please share anything that you like. Or, on the flip side, anything you don't want."

"The fireplace is attractive—and I could live with it—but I'd prefer a wood stove. I would be able to use wood to heat the house then."

Holly made notes as he spoke.

"Two-story ceiling, wood floors, open kitchen. All good."

He added, "I won't send anyone to the ER, but I'm just an adequate cook. A chef's kitchen isn't one of my requirements."

Holly glanced up from her phone. The next question would be awkward no matter what, but worse now that she personally wanted to know. Not that she'd be unfaithful. "Okay, what about the woman in your life? Does she enjoy cooking?"

When silence greeted her question, she looked up to find him staring at her. "I'm sorry. I don't want to be too personal with you. That's a question I would ask anyone on a tour like this."

He brushed her comment aside. "I guess I'm sensitive about it. I'm over thirty, and my mother hasn't stopped asking for a 'daughter to love like her own.'" He said the last part in a high voice and fluttered his eyelashes.

This man in front of her couldn't be the same one she'd spent all those hours listening to in school. And he didn't have a wife or girlfriend? "You should be like this in class."

He shook his head. "I need to appear professional in class."

She shrugged. "Professors are people too. Of course, you'd have the female portion of the student body standing in line to take your class if you were yourself."

"Really?" He gave her a slow, sexy smile that started to curl her toes, but she pushed those traitors back down. No toe curling allowed with clients.

"Whew. I should *not* have said that. I apologize for crossing the line between professional and personal."

He started for the stairs, glancing over his shoulder for a second. "Don't worry about it. I'll take your words to heart. I've only been a full-time professor a few years, and I'm not much older than most of my students. I want to be taken seriously. Maybe I'm trying too hard."

She followed him up the stairway to the second story that overlooked the great room below. At the top, she said, "The master is to the right, the guest room and Nathaniel's office are to the left."

She followed Dr. O'Connell when he went to the right and into her sister's master bedroom. "Jemma lightened up what was a dark, man-cave of a bedroom."

He went through the bedroom to a window that overlooked the back of the property. Instead of a frown when he pulled back drapes, he sighed. "Beautiful and peaceful."

"Remember, he built this house on property he found after searching for months. Are you open to building?"

Dr. O'Connell released the drapes but stood in the same position for a few seconds as the fabric fell straight. Turning, he said, "I've considered going that direction, but I'm a man without a home right now. I don't know if I want to wait that long."

Holly felt her brow furrow. "Didn't you tell me just this morning that you were living near the Jackson's house?" At his blank stare, she added, "The house I've been cleaning up."

He nodded. "Yes, but also remember that I said it was temporary." He looked heavenward for a moment. "Please God, only a short time longer." He continued toward the door.

"Why are you there?" She waved her hand in front of her face. "Sorry. That isn't any of my business."

Dr. O'Connell went into what Holly knew was a well-appointed master bathroom, coming back out a minute later. "My story isn't a secret. In fact, it was on the news. The townhouse I'd lived in since moving to Anchorage caught fire. Mine and others in the building." He checked his watch. "Twenty days ago, in fact."

"I remember reading about that! Did you lose everything?"

"Nothing that can't easily be replaced. My dog and I were in Kenai for the weekend. I lost clothing, furniture, kitchen supplies, which—"

"Don't matter to you." Holly grinned.

"Not overly much. Finals week was coming up, and I needed a quick place to stay so I could finish the semester. Another professor offered his guest room."

"That was nice of him, right?"

"A blessing. But I need to move out. Soon. Very, very soon."

"Because there isn't a decent place for your dog?"

"No. She's staying with my parents in Kenai because I thought she'd be happier there until I found our new home. I don't like to speak badly of someone who's been kind, but I'm not sure how much more of living with Tim I can take." He rubbed his hand over his face the same way he had when they'd spoken about this earlier in the day. "I share his guest room with a set of drums."

Holly fought, but didn't manage to win, against the grin that spread across her face. "And he plays them sometimes?"

"That's just it. I might be able to take occasional drumming. These drums come to life once a week when his band—really a group of aging hippies—stops by for practice. *Every* Saturday night. I learned the first week.

Now I visit my parents every weekend to avoid the chaos and late-night revelry. My visits make my dog happy, but it means I lose a lot of real estate searching time. Tim and I were new friends when this started less than a month ago, and our friendship's been strained. The drum beats from that first night—one I spent half of on the living room couch—still reverberate in my head. I must buy a home *soon*."

She tried and failed to picture someone conducting a practice session in her bedroom. "Having people in my room when I wasn't there wouldn't feel right."

"No. And when I returned last Sunday, I found a paper plate with pizza crusts on it in my closet. Someone must have stashed it there when he needed space to do whatever it is a band member does."

Holly thought through the calendar. "But today's—"

"Saturday. I know. I'm here because I need to find a house as soon as possible. Tonight, I'll be at my parents' house."

She stepped toward the guest room. "Hold on, didn't you say your parents live in Kenai? That drive is in the neighborhood of three hours."

"I'm not planning to drive. I'll fly."

"You own a plane?"

"I do. I'll fly back to Kenai after we're done."

"What about tomorrow?"

"I'll gladly fly back tomorrow if it gets me into a house of my own sooner." She'd lived in Alaska only a short time when it had become clear that many pilots saw their planes as akin to a car, a simple means for getting from point A to point B—sometimes the only way to do so.

"It's a deal. Let me see if I can set up some showings."

"Don't bother anyone on Saturday night."

"Real estate agents work every day of the week and every hour they're awake. You'd be amazed at the number of times I've been called at ten at night by a client."

Dr. O'Connell continued out the door and toward the guest room. He paused in the guest room's entrance. "This room feels inviting." Inside, he went through to the attached bathroom.

"This was one of Jemma's first design projects. I'll tell her you appreciated her efforts."

"She's a home decorator?"

"As a sideline. At least, she started decorating as a sideline. She has a business flipping furniture."

Dr. O'Connell stared at her in a way that told her he might be picturing Jemma juggling end tables. "She buys old, unloved pieces of furniture and rehabs them, turning them into things she can sell. Her office is across the street." She went to the window and parted the blinds so he could see the house Jemma used to call home.

Peering through them, he said, "That's a cute old house."

"She said I could show it to you as another example. Do you think you'd be interested in a house the age of your grandmother?"

Moving away from the window, he said, "I'm coming to believe that the land is more important to me than the house that's sitting on it. I can change the house."

"Yes. There's that old real estate adage: Location, location, location. It won't be a problem to find houses on a bit of land. The question is, how far are you willing to drive to your work at the university?"

He sat on the bench in the corner of the room, so Holly perched on the edge of the bed.

"I started out thinking I wanted to be close to work. That's what the real estate agent showed me."

"You don't want that now, though?"

"No. I want this." He pointed to the window and the view beyond. "Dennis couldn't get regular subdivisions out of his mind. I decided he wasn't finding me what I needed, so I had to expand my search. And he kept showing me what I didn't want. The last house . . ." He shook his head. "It had a jet fly so close over it that it felt like it would land there."

Holly didn't ever make negative comments about another agent to a client—that made everyone look bad—so she simply said, "I'll do my best for you." Then she stood and crossed the room, heading out the door and to the landing that overlooked the great room, with Adam following behind and stopping beside her. Holly pointed at the open door of Nathaniel's office. "He's a marketing consultant who works from home."

Dr. O'Connell stepped into the room, glanced around, and returned. "An office I'd be happy to call my own."

"I've learned what I need to know about your perfect home." She flipped through the calendar in her phone. "I could spend tomorrow afternoon touring houses with you. If we find one, a thirty-day closing is standard for financing. Let's go downstairs and talk over the rest of the details about what you need and want in your and your dog's new home."

Seated at Jemma and Nathaniel's dining room table, Holly went through her list of easy questions first. Number of bedrooms: three, so he could have a guest room and office like this house did. Bathrooms: an attached master bath and at least one other bathroom on each floor.

Then she broached the subject of budget.

Her former professor answered with a figure higher than she'd expected from a professor's wages. At her startled look, he explained, "I have income from other sources."

She nodded. Investments were on her future list, the list that also included publishing a book. Both would probably wait for another decade.

He added, "And I could pay cash for the house."

Holly felt her chest tighten. How many people had hundreds of thousands of dollars in ready cash? Not many in her circle of friends. Well, no one in her circle of friends. As she searched for the right words to find out what investments he was in—and if she could get some of that action—the homeowners returned with an exuberant Chloe.

Adam could feel Holly's and Jemma's eyes on him as he walked toward his current mode of transportation, still parked at the house Holly planned to get ready for sale. Coming from a family with five boys, he knew he didn't fully understand the sister dynamic, but he had a strong feeling they were evaluating him.

When he glanced back at the front porch as he settled onto his motorcycle, they stopped talking. Holly adjusted her shirt collar in a nervous, fidgety manner while Jemma examined the doorbell. Yes, they'd been talking about him. Holly, his new real estate agent, smiled and gave a very professional wave as he started the engine.

Wheeling around toward the street, he drove off and was soon on the Glenn Highway heading back to Anchorage, a route all too familiar since the untimely demise of his rental.

He passed the Palmer Hay Flats, an area he'd explored when he'd moved to Anchorage the summer before. As the old name suggested, farmers had used the land as hay fields. The massive 1964 earthquake had dropped the land a couple of feet and turned it into wetlands.

Beyond the Hay Flats, he drove past Fire Lake on his left, noting the float planes resting on it. He'd tried flying a float plane once, but greatly preferred the feeling of solid ground under him as he landed. Closer to Anchorage, a sign for Eagle River directed drivers to the next off-ramp. Maybe that could be his answer for a new home. The drive to Anchorage couldn't be more than twenty or thirty minutes. If it checked out, he'd call Holly and ask her to try that direction first.

Taking the ramp, he then made a left onto the Old Glenn Highway and proceeded into Eagle River. Groceries, fast food, a small hotel—nothing that spoke to him and said he could have his own slice of nature. He shook his head. Coming to view houses here would result in another failed search if this was anything to go by. He followed signs to re-enter the highway and continued toward Anchorage.

His years in grad school, all spent in big cities, had gotten him used to grocery stores and everything else being close by. But the constant busyness of a city like Chicago or Atlanta, or even Anchorage, left him feeling more than a bit stressed out at times. He'd liked Anchorage better though because he was so close to nearby nature when he'd lived there. But that wasn't enough anymore. Coming home to Alaska had brought back some of the small-town boy in him.

He took an exit to his right and headed for his university office. They'd be powering up instruments at Tim's right now, so he couldn't get any work done there. After that, he'd fly to his parents' house for the night. Blue sky with a few small white clouds gave him the go-ahead for his plans.

Chapter Seven

Holly threw an open box of brightly-colored cereal into a trash bag, then reached for a half-used bag of flour.

Bree came out of the downstairs powder room wearing yellow rubber gloves, her arms bent at the elbows and her hands upright in the classic doctor just-washed position. "All clean. Could you check it over to make sure I cleaned it to your standards? If it's a yes, I'll do the upstairs bathrooms."

"It's perfect."

"And you know that without looking because . . .?"

Holly set a can of soup on the counter. "You're a doctor, and I've watched you clean. I could eat off the floor in there." She grimaced. "Not that I plan to."

Jemma stepped away from cleaning sticky kid fingerprints off the stair railing and peered into the small room. Holding her hand in front of her eyes, she acted like she was shielding them from the sun. "Good call. It sparkles."

Holly's phone chimed three times, signaling a text from Matt. Picking it up, she read his message. *On my way. See you in twenty.* "Matt's coming over to help. I'd texted him about this project, but I thought he was still in the Bush."

Jemma raised her eyebrow. "Ooh. Should we go and leave the lovebirds alone?"

Thinking about the lack of steam on their last several dates, Holly leaned her elbows on the island. "I don't think that will be necessary."

Both sisters came over to the kitchen island and sat on the stools that remained in front of it—the only furniture left in the house. They grouped the stools so they faced each other, and Holly came over and took hers.

Jemma motioned toward herself with her hands. "Give. Tell us what's wrong."

Holly blew out a breath. "It isn't so much that something is wrong. But it doesn't seem like he's interested in ramping up our relationship."

"Just friends?"

Their brief goodnight kisses were just above a handshake. But, on the other hand, they weren't a handshake. "I don't know what to believe." She shrugged. "Sometimes he adds a little more oomph to the kiss. Other times, he seems very thoughtful, and I wonder if he's about to propose."

"Do you want him to propose?"

Holly had lain in bed last night, staring at the ceiling, picturing the four of them as a happy family. The image came easily to her. They'd do fun, outdoorsy things, the two adults and the girls. "He'd be a great father for Abbie and Ivy."

Bree became serious, morphing into Dr. Briana Harris in front of Holly's eyes. "I want my nieces to have a wonderful father figure in their life, but what does their mother say about a permanent relationship with Trooper Cooper?"

"He would always treat me nicely."

"Good."

Jemma and Bree glanced at each other, each wearing the same concerned expression.

Bree continued, "Do you want to share your life with him?"

The image shattered. "I don't know. He's . . . nice. I like being with him. But sometimes I feel like his buddy."

Dr. Bree vanished as her sister giggled. "Don't be upset about being his friend. Being friends with your husband before you're married makes the marriage—or I should say the honeymoon—more of a wow."

Holly felt her mouth drop open and saw her sister Jemma's do the same. Bree's face went from the fair skin typical of someone with reddish hair to a bright pink; then she broke eye contact with them. Holly pointed at Bree.

Jemma nodded slowly. She and Holly spoke at the same time.

Holly said, "You didn't—"

Jemma said, "Is there something we don't—?"

Jemma waved a hand toward Holly. "You first."

"I'm surprised I'm asking this because I *know* you wouldn't get married without having your family present, but it's either that or there's some pre-marital hanky-panky going on, and you said you weren't going to do that."

Her words met silence. Holly followed Bree's gaze to the ceiling of the room. The cobweb in the corner couldn't hold her sister's, or anyone's, interest this long.

Finally, Bree turned back toward them. "I had to stay in a hotel every time we went to New York. We didn't want to share his home because that might have led to . . ."

Holly raised her right eyebrow. "We get the picture. And?"

Bree rushed her words. "And we had a small ceremony in the chapel of our church in New York with a couple of his friends as witnesses."

Holly stood. "You what?" she said louder than she'd intended.

Bree winced. "We're going to have our large family wedding this summer."

"And you hadn't planned to tell anyone you were already married?"

"Well . . ."

"Should we be mad or hug her?" Jemma asked Holly.

Bree slid off her stool and held her arms wide. "Hugs, please?" Both sisters stood, and Bree pulled them close for a group hug.

When they stepped back, Bree reached into the purse she'd set on the kitchen island and pulled out a ring with a row of large diamonds set in a simple, but elegant, band. She slipped it onto her left ring finger, the stones catching the light.

Holly stared in amazement at her sister's hand. "Whew. Those are massive diamonds. When you didn't want an engagement ring, only a wedding ring, I expected a plain gold band."

Jemma held onto Bree's hand and leaned in to see the ring. "Michael chose well."

Bree's gaze swept up to meet Jemma's. "How did you know he chose it?"

Letting go of her sister's hand, Jemma shrugged. "Easy. You wouldn't select diamonds that big—maybe not a diamond at all. He can afford it, and he's a smart guy, so he made sure the stones were all set low so they wouldn't catch things when you're doing your doctor duties."

Bree turned her hand from side to side as she watched her ring. Sighing, she held her hand to her chest. "He did choose well."

Holly laughed. "The question is, do we tell Mom and Dad you're married?"

"The people I've worried most about not telling before the wedding are our grandparents. Especially Mom's mom, Grandma Eleanor. She met Michael last summer, so there's more of a connection there."

"She won't be happy about the little lapse in sharing."

"But she's always forgiven me for my social errors in the past. Remember when I forgot to send thank you cards for medical school graduation gifts? She wasn't happy when her sister mentioned she hadn't received one."

"Livid is more like it. I remember Grandma's expression when she stepped off the plane on her next visit. And this is somewhat of a larger social error." When Bree seemed near tears, Holly added, "But she loves you, and she'd rather have her first great-grandchild be the product of a married couple than not."

Jemma laughed. "Yes, play that card if she seems upset. She'll soon get over it." She hugged Bree one more time.

Bree slipped off her ring and stowed it in her purse.

Holly asked, "Now that we know—"

"Because I don't want it damaged while I clean." Bree went over to the sink and grabbed the rubber gloves she'd dropped in it earlier. "Two more bathrooms to go. I have to hurry so I can get out of here at four."

"I have to thank you two for helping. And Nathaniel and his brother earlier. It will be finished tonight. I may be shampooing carpets at 2 a.m., but I'll be able to put the listing up tomorrow and, I hope, sell it soon." Matt's ringtone sounded. A call instead of text was a rarity. "Matt, is everything okay?"

"Yes. I wondered if there's anything you need me to pick up on the way."

A stain on the carpet caught her eye. "Could you stop and pick up a rental carpet shampooer and some of the liquid cleaner that goes into it?" She'd be able to get started on the rugs even earlier then.

"I have plenty of time to do that. I just got called into work tonight to a Valley location, so I can't stay after all." He paused so long that she held her phone out to see if the call had dropped. "I actually called to ask you to dinner Monday night."

Why had he hesitated? "I'd like to go to dinner."

"Great," he said in a tone that seemed both happy and formal. Strange, but Holly hoped she'd get answers when she saw him.

Setting her phone down, she found both sisters watching her. She pointed at her phone. "Matt."

"And?" Jemma asked.

Holly screwed up her face as she tried to put what had happened into words. She shrugged. "He'll be here soon. You two can try to figure it out. You're the men experts in the house."

"Ha!" Jemma said. "Does anyone ever become an expert on the opposite sex?"

Bree picked up a bottle of cleaner. "As a newlywed of only a few weeks, that makes me feel better. You are the expert."

Jemma poked her chest with her thumb. "Six months into marriage, I can hardly call myself an expert."

Holly lifted one shoulder. "You've made it longer than I did. I'm going to wipe out the cupboards, then start on the fridge."

Jemma grimaced. "I didn't want to do the fridge, so I'm glad you assigned me to the upstairs." She moved in that direction. "I'm getting out of here before you change your mind."

Holly opened the appliance's door. "I think they were a normal family before their troubles. Too bad they lost control of their house afterward. You could get some samples for Petri dishes from this thing, Bree. Maybe students would discover a new strain of something."

Bree leaned around the side of the fridge. "Open the windows before you dive into this thing. I'd tell you to wear a mask, but I doubt you have one."

"Nope." Holly swung the door shut.

Holly's middle sister vanished up the stairs, leaving her to take care of the cupboards and build up courage for the fridge.

"If I were a successful mystery author selling a thousand books a month, I wouldn't ever have to do this again. Or show someone eighty-nine houses only to have them go in another direction." She set the cleaning spray and paper towels on the island.

As she stared at the fridge, dreading the next hour of her life, a handsome dark-haired man in a uniform opened the door. His biceps bulged and stretched the fabric as he effort-lessly carried the carpet shampooer in one hand and the cleaning solution in the other.

"Matt, thank you for getting that. You've saved me time." Holly reached for her purse. "Let me write you a check."

He waved her comment away. "Just consider it my contribution to the project." He glanced around. "The house is looking good. I wish I could stay and help."

Something that felt a little like love rushed through her. She didn't tingle, and her toes didn't curl. Maybe it was a strong case of like. As she watched him fill the reservoir on the cleaner, she felt what women throughout time had when they'd seen a man in uniform. What was the special attraction? When he stood, she pasted on a neutral expression.

"Duty calls. I need to be on the job in about ten minutes."

"Going to keep Alaska safe from criminals?"

"I'm doing what I can. I'll be in the Valley until late though, so I'll swing by and pick it up whenever you call." When he turned for the door, he added, "Dress up on Monday. I thought we could go somewhere nicer, maybe in Anchorage."

As he opened the door, she called out, "How dressed up?"

He seemed to ponder her question, finally coming up with a guy answer. "I've heard a little black dress mentioned in movies. That sounds about right. I have something important to say that night."

She nodded as he left and closed the door behind himself. Then she swung back around when Jemma said, "I heard that." Her sister leaned over the upstairs railing.

"Me too." Bree stepped beside Jemma. "A proposal?"

Holly tapped the top of the machine he'd dropped off. "Does a carpet cleaner say romance?"

"Do you want him to propose?"

Holly's phone rang, saving her from trying to formulate an answer to the question that seemed to be hanging in the room. She didn't have a clue. Her mother's picture filled the screen, letting her know she'd get to talk to her girls.

"Mommy!" the voice she'd know anywhere as her Abbie's said as soon as she answered.

Ivy immediately chimed in. "We're having fun!"

The muttering of an older voice in the background could barely be heard. Just as she was about to ask the person to speak up, Ivy added, "And we miss you."

Holly laughed. The fun had overwhelmed Ivy's need for her mother. That made her sad and glad. She wanted her girls to be able to stand on their own. Just not yet. The call lasted about ten minutes, each girl detailing what they'd done that day in Fairbanks. Together they said, "We love you!" before her mother came on the line and told her all was well. After the call ended, Holly stared at her phone. Promised photos of the day arrived, and she flipped through them.

Jemma leaned over to see. "I bet they're having a great time."

"I know. I just wish I was there with them instead of doing this." She motioned to the room around her.

Jemma pointed at the phone. "Wow, is that the time? I need to get out of here soon. I'd better tell Bree because she needs to go back to Anchorage before dinnertime."

Holly watched her head up the stairs. Both sisters both had plans for the evening. A date with cleaning supplies stretched in front of her. *Whoopie.* She slipped on her rubber gloves as she prepared for more fun. Fridge first, then she'd have to figure out the carpet cleaner—a machine she'd never been this close to before.

Jemma and Bree pounded down the steps a few minutes later, each hauling their cleaning supplies over to the kitchen island.

Bree gave Holly a hug. "Sorry to run out on you, sis."

"Have a great night with Michael."

Jemma reached over for a hug. "I can come back after church tomorrow if you don't finish."

"I'll finish. I may be a bit groggy sitting in the pew, but I'll finish."

When her two sisters filed out the door, Holly added, "And Bree, please tell the rest of the family you're married. I don't want to be the one to slip up and give it away."

"Me neither," Jemma added. She made a point of turning the lock on the door before closing it.

"What have I gotten myself into?" Holly asked the empty room. She'd never even plugged in a carpet cleaner, much less used one, so she didn't know how long the process would take.

She picked up her clipboard. Jemma had entered the house earlier, carrying it along with a printout she'd created with the tasks to be completed listed. She'd said, "I may have missed a few, but I thought this could keep us on track."

Jemma's planning skills were legendary.

Holding the clipboard where she could read it, Holly had said, "I'll see if this helps." Scanning the list, she'd known it would. She might make fun of her sister's "plans," but if Jemma suggested this for working more efficiently, she'd try it.

Holly now went down that checklist. She needed to make sure she was on track. The fridge came on right then, reminding her that the worst was yet to come. A walk-through of the whole property might help. Starting outside, she noticed that one of her helpers had pulled weeds out of what had been a flower bed sometime in the past. She crossed that off the list. The lawn had an air of neglect, but she'd have to live with it. Maybe a couple of pots with bright flowers would distract buyers.

Around back, she found nothing amiss, so she went inside the garage through a back door. Her sisters' husbands had done an excellent job in here. Husbands? She stopped where she stood. Holly Harris remained the lone single female in her family. Even her widowed grandmother had found a man last year. Maybe Matt would offer a change in her marital status, beginning with Monday's dinner.

As she closed and locked the door, she mentally checked her closet for his requested little black dress. If that phrase was so well known that all-male Matt Cooper had heard of it, she needed to add one to her closet, a closet that currently contained a single dress appropriate for a fancier dinner out. The teal dress suited her, but it wasn't black. Jemma, a.k.a. she-who-had-an-amazing-wardrobe, would have what she needed. Receiving a clothing allowance during her years as a corporate executive assistant had blessed her oldest sister with a closet—make that *closets*—filled with designer evening and business wear.

Holly entered the house through the garage and crossed to the downstairs powder room. You could eat off the various surfaces in the bathrooms Bree had cleaned. As a single, working mother of two young girls, she didn't have time to devote to spotlessness.

Upstairs, they'd emptied the bedroom closets. She'd found a disaster area when she'd crawled through the upstairs window yesterday morning—had it been that recently?—but the paint on the walls didn't seem damaged. Once the carpet was cleaned, the house would look close to new. And bring in a *much* higher sales price and profit to her when it sold.

Chapter Eight

Whistling, Adam hopped on his motorcycle in the university's lot and began the short drive to Merrill Field. He'd tried to work, but visions of the lovely Holly Harris had filled his mind instead. At first, she'd been a pretty face in his class. When he'd seen her mind at work through her assignments, he'd been intrigued. Meeting her again because of his temporary stay in small-town Palmer was the one good thing to come out of the fire.

His conclusion: pursue a relationship with her. Begin with friendship, and work up slowly to asking her out.

Almost to the airport, the bright sunshine became filtered, then disappeared as he neared his plane. A study of the sky didn't make him want to get into a plane's cockpit. Charcoal-gray clouds had pushed over the sun and begun to fill the area overhead. At his plane he checked his phone, and he found that the storm's predicted arrival time had sped up by a day.

True to form, Alaska's unpredictable weather left him with a problem. His plane wouldn't be leaving the ground today. He'd taken off a few years ago when the sky had seemed on the edge of all right and had almost immediately regretted his decision, kissing the ground when he'd safely landed at his destination.

Flying to Kenai was out. Driving there would involve riding a motorcycle through a storm for hours. Truth be told, he'd been a sunny day motorcycle rider before his car had been totaled. Plowing through the rain with nothing but a leather jacket, jeans, and boots to protect him from the storm didn't sound like a plan he wanted to embrace.

He could rent a car and go to Kenai. That would be a long drive both ways that he could avoid. Emma would miss him, but a hotel or a friend's couch were his best options. The hotel, not usually his favorite housing option, appealed most to him tonight—maybe one with a nice restaurant inside, so he didn't need to get anywhere near his motorcycle in the rain.

Flying back to Palmer tomorrow would be a no if the longevity of the weather front proved accurate. He punched in the number for the lovely Holly Harris to postpone tomorrow's appointment. Letting her down royally messed up his plans to spend time with her. But he didn't see a choice. At least it wasn't a date, so she wouldn't think he'd stood her up. And, for all he knew, she was dating someone else.

She answered on the fourth ring, frustration singing down the line. Her reply to his postponement sounded infused with panic. "I'm sure I can find a property for you."

"Holly, this isn't about your skills. A storm's rolling in and my set of wheels are just that—two tires and no cover. Beyond that, I can't fly back to my parents' house, so I'm going to have to find a hotel room for the night. I'll just stay in Anchorage."

Her reply to his words was filled with relief. "That's probably best. I have to finish up this house anyway and get it on the market."

"I thought you said you'd be done today."

"This is more information than I should give a client, but the carpet cleaner and fridge say otherwise. I'll be here until long after midnight."

He paused as he considered his options. Assist the fair maiden, or be certain he'd stay warm and dry? The fair maiden won. "Can I help with anything?"

"Unless you're a pro at operating a carpet cleaner, I'm . . . okay."

He chuckled. "Actually, I am an expert with a carpet cleaner."

"Unlikely. Writing an essay about one won't help me." She sounded amused.

"No, I am a bona fide expert. I can clean carpets with the best of them."

"Instead of mowing lawns or delivering newspapers, as every boy in America seemed to do for extra money, you cleaned carpets." A smile wove in between her words.

"Ouch. You do have a sarcastic bent to you. My parents owned several rental houses, and every time someone left, we'd have to clean, paint, whatever, and get it ready for the next tenant. I apparently outshone my brothers with the tedious task of cleaning the carpets."

"So you learned to love the fine art of bringing carpet back to life."

"No." He sighed dramatically. "I have to admit to painting envy. My older brother was tasked with painting, and I wanted to do that. I would hurry through my job, making sure I did it well, so Dad didn't make me do it again. Then I would help paint."

"You ground yourself farther into the expert hole by being efficient and fast."

"You see my dilemma." He caught himself. Helping her tonight was out of the question unless he went to a hotel in Palmer.

His pause communicated his feelings. Frustration tinged her sigh. "I wish you *could* help."

"I'm going to get a hotel room here in Anchorage."

"Right, because you can't fly to Kenai either. But you're *willing* to help me, right?"

Her sadness reached into his heart. "Sure."

Holly leaned back against the kitchen island. "I have an idea. Can you wait where you are for a few minutes while I check on it?"

The sound of a loud engine revving came through the line as she waited for his response. He must have stopped by a busy road. The noise lowered before he replied. "Just a few minutes. Then I'm going to have to find a place to stay."

She ended the call and dialed Jemma, panic surging through her. Postponing showings meant postponing a sale. Worse yet, he might choose to work with another agent or return to the old one. She and Dr. O'Connell had spent less time working together than he had with that man. Maybe he felt loyal to him after all.

Take a deep breath, Holly. Dr. O'Connell needed a room and a ride. Her house had an empty room with two twin beds in it, but that would be inappropriate beyond words. Jemma had a guest room. Better than that, she had rooms upstairs in her old house that weren't used right now. She and Nathaniel had considered making the place into a bed and breakfast but had put that concept on hold.

Her sister answered on the fourth ring. "I'm here, Holly. Don't hang up."

"Are you okay?"

"Sure. You caught me in the middle of sawing the top off a dilapidated desk so it can be born again as a marble-topped storage unit. I turned off the jig saw just in time to hear the ring. What's up?"

She explained the situation at the house Dr. O'Connell temporarily called home and about the weather report. "He doesn't have a place to spend the night. I can't show him houses tomorrow if he isn't around."

Jemma said, "He'd probably be more comfortable in Great-aunt Grace's place instead of having us down the hall. I'll be finishing up in my shop in another hour so it should be quiet. He's welcome to stay. I might even be able to talk Nathaniel into making one of his special Sunday breakfasts for him in the morning."

"The blueberry coffee cake?"

Jemma laughed. "I think we still have some berries in the freezer from last fall. Perhaps."

Holly's mouth started to water. "Let me know when to be there." She held the phone away and saw that several minutes had passed. "I'd better call Dr. O'Connell back now."

"Does he call you Ms. Harris?"

"Don't get started on me. That man is permanently in my mind as a professor. First names are for friends."

"See you soon."

Holly dialed her client back. "You've got a room at my sister Jemma's for the night."

"Awesome! I'm not a huge fan of hotels. I hope you can find a house like theirs for me."

"Not at that house. The one across the street." She hurried to add, "You can stay in the new house, but you'd have the older house to yourself for the night. We thought you'd like that."

Silence greeted her again. A sound she now realized was an airplane was the only indication the call hadn't dropped. "If you're sure? You're willing to let a virtual stranger stay there?"

"Of course."

"Then I can't thank you enough!"

"Call me when you're almost to Jemma's. I'll run over and pick you up so you don't have to ride in the rain when we're done."

"Thanking you is becoming a habit. I don't have a change of clothes with me. I'd counted on those at my parents' and don't want to interrupt music practice, so I hope I beat the storm." He hung up, leaving her staring at her phone. She needed to forget her needs and find this man the house of his dreams soon—for his sake, not just hers.

Adam checked the reservoir of the carpet cleaner Holly had rented and found it almost empty. He opened the bottle of cleaning liquid beside the machine and poured it in.

He still wasn't sure why he was here when he could have checked into a hotel, had a nice dinner, and maybe taken a walk before the storm hit. Holly glanced up from wiping out a cupboard and smiled at him.

Now he remembered. She'd sounded sad and stressed-out on the phone when he'd called to cancel Sunday's showings. She'd been cleaning, and his mouth had opened to say he'd help. The internal tug to help her had overruled his relaxation plans. Sure, his parents had raised five boys who helped others, but Holly felt special.

A box of chocolates sat on the kitchen counter, something his dad always bought when his mother needed cheering up. Holly had pounced on that box like it provided sustenance after a week with nothing to eat. Watching her savor the first piece—the way her expression calmed for a fleeting moment—had made the stop at the store worthwhile.

She selected another piece from the box, holding it up. "Thank you for this."

"You said you liked chocolate."

Her face screwed up in confusion. "When?"

"Right before your shoe hit my head."

Holly grinned, just about knocking him off his feet. "But you really scored with a box of *dark* chocolate."

"Every woman I've known prefers dark chocolate."

She raised an eyebrow. "Really?"

"My mother, fellow students . . ."

She didn't break her stare.

"And a girlfriend." A few seconds later, he lowered his voice and added, "Buying Melissa dark chocolate might have been the one thing I did right."

"I feel ready to move forward now." She picked up her paper towels. "And I'm sorry about Melissa." Glaring at the fridge, Holly pursed her lips. "Bree didn't exaggerate about the toxins in this cold, white box." Holly crossed the room to open a window and then a second one. She returned to the center of the kitchen, slipped her gloves on, and yanked a trash bag out of the box. Then another.

"There must be a lot of garbage in there.

"This will be a two-bag project, maybe three, by the time I've dumped in everything from the freezer. I sure wouldn't trust a bite of food in here." With that, her upper body disappeared into the appliance.

Recapping the bottle of cleaning fluid, he realized he would have bought her a case of chocolate and painted all night if that's what she'd needed. Besides, it didn't hurt that he was helping his real estate agent, a woman who held an important part of his future in her hands. He and Emma needed a place to call their own. Beyond his house hunt, he enjoyed being near Holly. Would she accept him as anything more than a professor?

This would be step one in his campaign to win the fair maiden's hand. Holly hadn't mentioned a man in her life. She wasn't his student anymore. All points in his favor. Helping her get through this day had to reflect positively back on him.

Not that he was a slimeball who would only help to get something from her. Her sad voice would have had him offering his services no matter who she was. The whole situation reminded him of how he'd gotten Emma. During graduate school, he'd overheard another student in a restaurant near the campus tell his lunch friend he had a puppy to give away, and that she wasn't the most attractive of the litter.

The man had found homes for the other puppies as soon as he could. His landlord didn't even know about the mother dog. If the ugly puppy didn't find a home, he'd drop her off at the animal shelter the next day.

Adam had finished his lunch, walked out the door and down the block with those words repeating in his head. What might happen to the little dog? The place he lived in allowed pets—at least he thought so based on the puppy chew marks on the edge of the door. He'd spun on his heels and reached the restaurant before the man had finished his meal.

One look at Emma and the adorable puppy with sad eyes had won his heart. When he'd picked her up, she'd snuggled close to him. They'd been inseparable ever since. Until this fire. No longer would an attached neighbor be able to make enough noise to wake the dead. He would own the whole building. Emma would have a yard to play in.

Now, he needed to find that place. He turned toward Holly. And work on more ideas to win her.

He couldn't let her know he was interested in her until *after* he'd bought the house. He didn't want her to be afraid to drive him around and show him places on her own, and coming on to her seemed a surefire way for that to happen. She might feel the need to pass him off to someone else in her office—a male real estate agent—if that were to happen.

It wouldn't. He could be a friend. Help her when needed. But he'd keep his distance until the moment after closing on his home.

Adam unrolled the cord and plugged it into an outlet on the living room's wall. "Is your career always this fun-filled, Holly?"

Holly threw a rag in the direction of the sink. "You've appeared on the scene during my most chaotic time. Until now, I've shown homes, sold them, listed homes, and sold those. Some people didn't buy, and one house didn't sell, so the owners rented it. But this? This one has been a challenge from the beginning." She sighed. "I probably shouldn't have agreed to clean it. My sisters questioned my sanity. Well, not really my sanity, but my judgment."

This would be a time when a sane man didn't say a word.

"I don't know why you've agreed to help, but thank you."

He bowed. "Damsel in distress. I've always been a sucker for one."

She grinned and picked up the bottle of cleaner. "Thank you."

Winning a second smile from Holly made the evening's efforts worthwhile. Now, he just needed to clean a couple thousand square feet of nasty, stained carpet. Turning the cleaner on, he started on a spot in the corner—grape juice, if he wasn't mistaken.

Two hours later, he could see the light at the end of the cleaning tunnel. Downstairs was done. He'd made his way upstairs by cleaning the steps, and two of the three bedrooms and the hallway were as close to new as he could get them. Holly found him in the last of the kids' rooms, pouring more fluid into the machine for the grand finale.

"You're a miracle-worker! Thank you! I watched you work and realized it would have been about ten o'clock tomorrow morning before I finished. And I'd have been exhausted." She blew out a big breath. "More exhausted than I am right now, and that's saying a lot."

"I'm happy to help. Professors have time on their hands during break. And it isn't as though I can go relax in my own place."

"For this, I'll find the right house for you. Hold it. I would have done that anyway. How about I get you a talented decorator for free?"

"Now you have my attention. I did my townhome in Early Bachelor."

"Brown, gray, nothing on the walls? Two plates and a bowl in the cupboard?"

"I'll have you know that I bought an entire set of dishes at the superstore. I had four of each."

"But the rest is right?"

"I hung my diploma in my office. That's art."

Holly gave a slow grin. "Jemma will help."

"Didn't she do the guest room at her house? The one that was pretty and a little country?" Definitely not his taste.

"Don't worry. She can do other styles. You can see what she did in Bree's fiancé's condo in Anchorage. I think you'll be happy."

"Will she agree to this arrangement?"

"Yes. Believe me. She'll enjoy decorating."

"I accept."

Rain pelted down on the front of the house. "Windows!" Holly pointed to the front of the house, and they both raced over to close them.

Once done, Adam cupped his hands on a window to see outside. "Definitely not motorcycle weather."

"If it isn't too personal, why not buy a car?"

Grinning, he stepped back. He liked her interest in his life. "I don't mind personal questions."

"I just wondered why you keep driving a motorcycle—if you don't like driving it in the rain. Surely your insurance will cover a new car."

"Where would I keep it? Until I'm back in a place of my own, I don't have anywhere to store a car *and* a motorcycle. I have to park in Tim's side yard as it is." Glancing at the carpet cleaner in front of him, he said, "When we leave here, I can help you return this to the place you rented it."

Holly stared at the machine. "I almost forgot. A . . . friend brought it over and said he'd pick it up. I'll text and let him know I'm done with it. I'm beyond ready to leave here." She headed out the door with a tense expression on her face. "I hope I can reach him."

Adam turned the machine on and finished up his work. Truth be told, his work here had taken longer than he expected, but he did have a place nearby to go for the night. One without live music.

As he carried the cleaner down the stairs, three chimes sounded on Holly's phone. She checked the text and said, "He says he'll be here in five minutes." Setting down her phone, she waved game show style at the fridge. "Just like new. I'm done here too."

Stepping toward the stairs, she said, "I'm going to make sure all the lights are off." He watched her go up them, then heard movement overhead. The doorbell rang as she was on her way back down.

Adam took the three steps to the door and opened it to find Holly's friend, a man wearing an Alaska State Trooper uniform. The newcomer's gaze went from Adam to Holly and back. He put out his hand. "Matt Cooper."

Adam shook it and introduced himself. Something about Cooper's attitude said that he was more than a casual friend. In fact, enough tension filled the room that you could have sliced through it.

Holly hurried down the rest of the stairs. "Matt, thank you for coming so quickly."

He gave her a smile that made her blush. Adam wanted to wipe that smile off his face. The reaction surprised him. He'd never been the jealous type in the past.

"I'm glad I was nearby." Matt turned to Adam. "Stakeout."

Adam pointed at the machine. "Cleaning."

Holly stepped between them. "I'm surprised you could leave your work, Matt."

He shrugged. "We've been on this detail for a while. I left another man on-site, and I'm picking up a late dinner for the two of us." He reached for the carpet cleaner, hefting it with one arm. Adam's physique couldn't compete with Cooper's muscles, so he prayed Holly didn't prefer muscle-bound men.

"Thank you again, Matt." She waved.

He nodded. "I'll see you soon." Turning, he gave Adam another male stare, then headed out the door, pulling it closed with his free hand.

Holly laughed nervously. "I can take you to Jemma's now, Adam. We'll look at houses tomorrow afternoon."

So wrapped up his first evening with Holly.

Chapter Nine

"How did you sleep last night? Did you have visions of real estate dancing in your head?" Holly asked him the next morning at the table in Jemma and Nathaniel's house. She'd dressed for church in black pants and a grass-green, short-sleeved sweater.

"The best night's sleep I've had since my townhome burned. Our tour of neighborhoods yesterday didn't interrupt me." Adam turned to his hosts. "Thank you for taking a stranger into your midst."

He felt better this morning than he had for a while. Pushing his hair, still damp from a shower, off his forehead, he glanced down at the new pair of black jeans he wore, one of two they'd bought last night along with a few shirts, underwear, socks, and toiletries at a superstore on the way to his home for the evening.

Jemma said, "Holly explained the situation with the drums."

Adam shuddered. "Between the drums and the cat's litter box . . ."

"Litter box?" Jemma and Holly said at the same time. Holly set down her mug and stared at him.

Adam took a sip of his coffee. "I could live with it. I mean, the cat was there first, right? And you can't just move something like that. She's a pretty cat."

Nathaniel and Jemma turned to each other, a frequent movement he'd noticed among newlywed friends, but this time the action looked purposeful and not just loving.

Nathaniel focused his gaze on Adam. "Jemma and I discussed this last night. Her power tools and other aspects of her business make noise during the day, but only then. You're welcome to stay in that house until Holly finds the right one for you."

Adam's mug slipped. Holly reached both hands around it, setting it on the table.

"Sorry." He pointed at the mug. "I've been living in a nightmare these last few weeks. I hadn't realized just how much it had gotten to me until this moment. Knowing I don't have to go back there, that I can be somewhere quiet with only the occasional sound of a power tool during the day is . . . amazing. Thank you."

Nathaniel added, "Some days, the noise from Jemma's workshop feels unending. You're trying to work, and the sounds of hammering and power tools won't leave you alone."

Jemma's mouth dropped open.

Nathaniel grinned. "Then you get used to it and don't even notice."

Jemma smacked him on the arm. "We might not have met if I didn't have power tools."

Nathaniel laughed and leaned over to kiss Jemma on her cheek.

Adam pointed toward the older house. "But you lived across the street from each other."

"He"—Jemma set her hand gently on her husband's arm—"wasn't interested in a relationship."

"She sawed her way into my heart." The pair stared into each other's eyes for a moment.

Jemma, now blushing, broke eye contact. "Now, before Adam decides he wants to give this pair of newlyweds a wide berth and turn down our offer . . ."

Adam leaned back in his seat. "Not a chance. I'm taking you up on your offer."

"You might start dreaming power tool sounds if the search takes too long. I guess it will be a good incentive for Holly to find you a house."

A buzzer sounded. Nathaniel went over to silence it and pulled a pan out of the oven. "Blueberry coffee cake anyone? Eggs scrambled with bacon bits and topped with cheddar cheese are warming on a low burner." He took out plates, then a knife, and began slicing the cake.

The mouth-watering scents of cinnamon and blueberries drifted by. "Now I know I must be hallucinating. Is there a doctor in the house?"

"Not right now. Bree will probably be here later—if you're still feeling delusional." Holly grinned. It hit him in the gut every time she did that.

Adam said, "Jemma, please tell me you didn't get up early to make breakfast because of me."

Holly and Nathaniel burst into laughter. The two of them doubled over to the point that Holly leaned over the table and Nathaniel against the kitchen island. Jemma glared at them, then chuckled.

Holly gasped, "Sorry, Adam. Remember, Jemma doesn't cook?" She wiped her tearing eyes. "She also doesn't get up early."

Jemma crossed her arms over her chest. "Hey, I think I might be offended."

Nathaniel carried over two plates, setting one in front of his wife and the other in front of Adam.

Jemma shrugged. "But not enough to lose my appetite. Looks delicious, honey."

"Enjoy the blueberries. These are the last of the wild berries we picked last fall."

Adam sampled the cake. This morning and these people made up for a lot of what he'd been through. "Thank you, Nathaniel. And Jemma, for your support of the chef. I'm sure you must do dish duty."

She smiled, and Adam could see her appeal to Nathaniel. She glowed with a fresh beauty. Much like her sister Holly, but Holly had an inner strength he was seeing more and more of. Something told him Holly might have some stories to tell about her life.

Adam forked up another bite of eggs. "I make a delicious Irish breakfast, courtesy of lessons from my granny."

"I visited Ireland once on business." Jemma closed her eyes. "Breakfast was amazing. We had bacon, sausage, eggs, fried tomato, and soda bread with fresh butter and home-made jam."

"My granny was born there and believed it her duty to share her heritage with her grandchildren. She'd love this too though." He took another bite of coffee cake.

Jemma opened her eyes. "Agreed. Honey, your food is always wonderful."

As he drained his coffee cup after his blissfully quiet night, Adam felt like jumping and shouting about the change in his life from yesterday to today. "Thank you again for letting me stay here."

"At least you won't have to fly back and forth to Kenai so often now, Adam." Nathaniel reached over the island for a coffee pot and topped off Adam's mug.

"I'll need to visit my Emma at least once a week. She's been as unsettled by this as I have."

Holly stared at him, a fork halfway to her mouth. Jemma and Nathaniel sat frozen in their seats. Adam went over his words. What had he said wrong? "I couldn't ask you to let her stay here too." Trying to be friendly in what had become decidedly icy, he slid another bite of breakfast into his mouth.

Finally, Jemma broke the silence. "I'm sorry, but we wouldn't want an unmarried man and woman living in the same house. Call us old-fashioned, but that's how we feel."

A bite of coffee cake lodged in his throat. Coughing, he reached for his coffee. Holly pounded him on the back.

"Emma . . . dog," he gasped between breaths. Nathaniel set a glass of water in front of him, and he gladly gulped down half of it.

"She's what, Adam?" Jemma asked.

He took a deep breath, grateful for the air that filled his lungs. As he pulled his phone out of his pocket, he started to laugh. Once he'd found a photo he'd snapped the day before, he handed the device to Holly.

Grinning, she passed it to Jemma who checked it, then handed it to her husband.

Nathaniel said, "Emma's your dog." Returning the phone, he added, "Chloe enjoys being around other dogs, so she'd probably like to play with her."

"Adam, my old house has a fenced backyard, and we're used to having a dog inside too. Emma is welcome to stay with you."

He swallowed hard as he fought the emotions that surged through him. It seemed Holly understood when she pointed toward the front of the house and said, "There's a powder room over there if you'd like to freshen up."

He nodded gratefully and exited before he made a scene in front of these people whom he barely knew. Perching on the edge of the toilet, the one place to sit, he gained control again. He knew his parents would do the same for someone in his situation, but that didn't make this any less miraculous.

Standing, he took the half step to the sink and splashed water on his face. He'd also be able to spend more time around Holly, being across the street from her sister. Maybe he could convince her they should date. It wouldn't seem like he was making advances on his real estate agent, more like he was a friend.

Feeling like he could conquer the world, he opened the door and stepped into the middle of a conversation.

"Please don't be disappointed if Matt doesn't do what you expect tomorrow."

Matt was the muscle-bound state trooper who'd picked up the carpet cleaner.

Holly seemed undeterred. "He said he had important news."

"Nathaniel, tell her that many things could be *important*."

"Don't burst her bubble, Jemma. She knows him better than we do. She could be right."

Holly pushed back her plate, a bite of cake uneaten. "Matt's made time for this dinner; he's somehow cleared his schedule. He must have something serious to say. Last week he was in Dutch Harbor. I looked it up. It's as long of a flight from Anchorage to Dutch as it is to Seattle—three hours. The week before it was Dillingham. Both are far from roads and far from here. He's in this area now, probably won't be here too long before his work sends him elsewhere, and wants to see me."

Jemma put her hand on her sister's. "I'm glad he's making time for you. I just don't want him to break your heart, Holly. Once was enough."

He felt like he should announce his presence. But this man, Matt, clearly stood between him and his interest in Holly Harris. He needed to know as much as possible about the situation. Had she fallen so deeply for him that she couldn't be interested in anyone else? Or did he still have a chance at winning her?

"He can't break my heart, Jemma. I know that he'd be good with—" She glanced up and saw him standing there.

Adam cleared his throat. "I'm sorry if I'm interrupting an important conversation."

Holly brushed aside his comment with her hand. "We're fine. You know sisters."

Returning to the table, he stood behind his chair. "I have four brothers—no sisters. Once we leave the realm of fiction, the sister relationship baffles me. In fact, even in fiction, I'm sometimes baffled. *Little Women* is supposed to be a wonderful book and a classic I thought I should be familiar with, but I struggled through the sisterly femaleness of it."

"Five boys? I can't imagine that. Our dad had three girls and taught us to camp and fish. Did your mom teach you to cook?"

"Not like that." He gestured toward the one remaining slice of coffee cake in the pan on the island. He must have given it a longing glance because Nathaniel laughed.

His host said, "It's yours if you want it."

"My mother taught her boys to be polite, so I accept." He picked up the pan and brought it to the table, realizing all eyes were on him as he pushed his plate to the side and set the pan in front of him. He glanced up to find Holly's eyes sparkling with amusement. "I may have felt a little too comfortable, and acted as I would at my parents' house."

She laughed. "No, we want you to feel that way. Without company, I might have done the same thing."

Nathaniel leaned back in his chair. "It makes a cook's heart happy to have someone enjoy their baking."

Adam slid a bite of the cake into his mouth, washing it down with a sip of his coffee. "That was excellent. Thank you."

Holly pushed back from the table. "We're off to church. I have six showings scheduled for you this afternoon."

Adam got up and walked over to the wall of windows facing the backyard. Rain still came down. "If you don't mind, I'll tag along. I've had one shower this morning—I don't want another on the drive to Anchorage and my church."

The next morning, he found sun pouring through the living room's windows when he came down the stairs of his new home. The storm had passed. On the way home from church the day before, they'd decided to cancel the afternoon's showings. A home's exterior was too important to him to race by it on his way to the front door. Holly said she'd be busy today. He knew about tonight's date with the trooper, so she might be focusing on makeup, hair, and all the other things women did. Not that she needed anything extra with her natural beauty.

Jemma popped out of the kitchen when he reached the bottom step. "I skipped breakfast at home and came over here to start working." She held up a mug. "Cup of tea or coffee? I keep bagels here so I can also offer you the finest toasted bagel in town. I'm known for my breakfasts." When she grinned, he remembered what Holly had said about her cooking skills.

He took the last step into the living room. "Coffee. But you don't have to get it."

She waved away his comment. "It's no problem. Yes or no on the bagel?" She turned back toward her kitchen, and Adam followed behind.

Almost sure that no one could ruin a bagel, he said, "I won't turn down food."

"Nathaniel gave me tips on coffee-making, so you'll enjoy this. Make yourself comfortable." She pointed to a small, round table circled with chairs. A relaxed silence settled over the room as she worked. The Harris sisters were easy to be around. With the coffee on, she pulled a bag of bagels out of an old-fashioned bread box on the counter, removed one, sliced it, then slid it into the toaster. "Did you sleep well last night?"

A giant sigh pushed out of him. "Heavenly. The best I've slept since the fire. No cat or human interruptions. Both would happen at five or six every morning."

About the same time he could smell the coffee, his bagel popped up. Jemma took it out, placed it on a plate, and brought it to him. Then she went to the refrigerator, pulled out several containers, and brought them over. Butter, cream cheese, and strawberry jam, homemade from the type of jar it was in.

He pointed to the jar of jam. "Your handiwork?"

"Nervous?"

"Well, your family did say . . ." He let the thought drift off.

"No, to answer your question. Holly made that. She can cook."

"Well?" he asked as he spread cream cheese on his warm bagel.

"Better than well. Amazingly." Jemma filled her mug at the sink and put it in the microwave. When it dinged, she took out the mug, picked up a soggy-looking tea bag off a plate—she must have already used it once this morning—and dipped it into the water, a thoughtful expression on her face.

After adding some of the jam, Adam took a bite. The fresh strawberry flavor burst on his tongue and he savored the bite. Holly did have cooking talents. Siblings could be so different from one another.

Each of his brothers had gone their own direction with their careers. One owned a small jewelry store. He couldn't imagine anything further from being an English professor. Although he did have his side career, and that required some entrepreneurial skills. Sometimes more than he would have expected.

When Jemma took the tea bag out of her mug and turned toward him, her expression became more determined. Guessing the inner workings of the female mind had never been his specialty—as evidenced by his miserable dating track record—but if he made a guess, he'd say she appeared to be a woman on a mission. Did it bode well for him?

"Do you ever date students?"

He leaned back in his chair. Where was this going? "I have a firm policy of never dating students."

"Even when they're not a conventional student, closer to your age?"

He nodded firmly. "Even then." On solid ground now, he took another bite of his bagel.

"Soooo, if you'd been interested in one of your students, you would have ignored that."

Chewing then swallowing, he answered, "Yes."

"But if she entered your life after she'd graduated, you'd follow up on that interest."

Dread seeped into him. Was Jemma warning him away from her sister? He thought back over the times they'd been together. Had he offended one of the Harris sisters?

After taking a deep, fortifying gulp of coffee, he answered. "Yes, I would. And yes, I am interested in your sister."

Jemma giggled.

This wasn't going down as he'd expected.

"I thought so. Bree and I support your efforts."

Not at all as he'd expected. "But she's dating another man, isn't she?"

Jemma stood, went over to the coffee maker, and returned with the pot to top off his cup. "She is, and she isn't. We don't think he's going to stick around."

Maybe he did have a chance with the lovely Holly.

"But," she said as she set the pot back on its warming plate, "I didn't see any possibility of Bree and Michael being a couple, and they're married."

He cocked his head to the side. "I thought I'd heard they were engaged."

"Sort of." Jemma took a sip of her coffee. "It's still a secret, but between you and me and Holly, they got married. To prevent any unmarried hanky-panky." She raised her eyebrows.

Adam grinned but felt heat creep up his face.

"Remember that. Harris girls don't mess around before marriage."

Whew. That was a warning if he'd ever heard one. "Yes, ma'am. I agree with that principle." When his old girlfriend had wanted to live together, he'd said no. "Holly is safe with me."

She gave a single nod. Then she took her cup over to the sink and rinsed it out, setting it to the side. "I need to get to work. I apologize in advance, but this is a sawing and sanding day. There will be some noise."

"I'm planning to fly to pick up Emma today. If you're sure she can stay here?"

"Yes. I'm looking forward to meeting her." At that, she exited through a back door he hadn't paid much attention to before.

Adam rode his motorcycle to Anchorage, flew to Kenai, and picked up what little gear he had there. For the return flight, he put Emma in a dog carrier strapped to the plane's passenger seat.

As he flew back to Anchorage, however, he realized that he'd left Emma's dog carrier for the motorcycle at his parents' house. She always enjoyed riding on the back of the motorcycle, but she couldn't without her carrier. He'd buy a new one tomorrow. But today, he'd divert to the Palmer airport, and call someone in the Harris bunch to pick them up there.

Jemma's planning skills—"legendary" was the word Holly had used—meant that everyone's number was in his phone and their schedules noted. Holly had a client in Wasilla, but Nathaniel would be working at home. He dialed the number, and his new neighbor said he'd be happy to pick him up in a half hour.

Once Adam settled his dog, he'd get a lift back to the airport, fly the plane to Anchorage, and ride his motorcycle back. It made for a convoluted day, but it was doable. It also took his mind off the fact that Holly had a big date with Matt tonight.

When Jemma had shut down her business for the day and crossed the street to the home she shared with Nathaniel, Adam brought his laptop out of its bag and set it on her dining room table. He'd never been so glad about anything as he had for the automatic backups that had saved all the documents on his old computer—the water-logged, smoke-filled one that now rested in the landfill—to a cloud storage area. He'd bought this computer and put the same programs on it. But *nothing* about his temporary living situation had brought on a desire to write.

Tonight, he felt ready to dig back into his story. Science fiction fans compared his work to the great Ray Bradbury's, something that never failed to give him a sense of awe, and they gleefully plunked down money for his books. He wrote because he loved it just as much as he did teaching. But he also enjoyed the extra income. Holly had never asked why he had the financial means to offer a cash purchase. Maybe she thought college professors earned a high income from their teaching positions.

The fan base of his alter-ego A. T. Martin, a name created from his first and middle initials and his mother's maiden name, had grown to the point that he earned much more from his writing than he did from his teaching job. Staying anonymous hadn't always been easy, but it was essential. Not even his family knew his secret, and that situation had to continue. His mother was like a sieve when it came to holding onto secrets.

In his first job interview after graduation, he'd proudly mentioned his first book and received the cold shoulder for writing popular fiction instead of something literary. He hadn't been offered the job, and he'd kept silent about it ever since. Being a laughing stock in the education world wasn't in his plans.

His fans expected three or four books a year. He'd have to write every night for a couple of weeks not only to make up for lost time, but also to get back into the rhythm of writing. Reading through the last chapter he'd written, he got excited about the next one. Emma jumped onto his lap and curled up, both of them in their usual positions.

He paused, wondering how Holly's date with Matt was going. He couldn't change the situation, so he pushed them out of his mind and stepped into an alien landscape with characters he could control.

Chapter Ten

As Holly neared the restaurant, a couple holding hands stepped out and stopped in front of her. The woman held up her left hand, the sparkling stones on her ring finger catching the light. Holly stopped, smiling as the woman spontaneously spun around and kissed the man before the two moved away from the restaurant.

Tonight would be Holly's night too. When Holly picked up her pace again, the heel of one of her jeweled, high-heeled shoes caught in a crack in the sidewalk. Grabbing for the side of the building, she steadied herself.

The shoes, the dress, the earrings she wore—everything except her undergarments—came from Jemma's legendary wardrobe. Their heights varied slightly, but their overall build was close enough for many of the items to work. Both she and Bree shopped their sister's closet for special occasions, and this one was as special as they came.

Jemma had taken photos of her as she had gotten ready to leave so she could remember everything about the evening.

Then she'd sent them to Bree so she could feel part of the event too.

Those same sisters didn't believe she should marry a man for the lone reason that he would be a good father to her kids. But Matt would also make a caring husband. She was sure of that. Well, she expected him to be a caring husband. He had a job where he chose between good and evil all day long. Surely, he'd know how to choose good for her.

Cars passed beside her on the busy street, reminding her how close she was to her car if she wanted to scurry back to it. When Matt had texted earlier that day and asked her to meet him an hour's drive away in Anchorage, the scenario hadn't fit her expectations of a grand evening. She'd pictured him knocking on her door and escorting her to his car. He'd immediately added that he had a meeting in Anchorage's trooper headquarters, would change there, and could still be on time that way.

They'd dated for more than half a year. He'd always been kind and considerate. They would have more in the beginning of their marriage than some did. With a single nod, she decided to move forward and not look back.

Their special dinner tonight in an expensive restaurant she'd never before dined at bore little resemblance to their usual dates at casual restaurants. Pushing open the door, Holly stepped into what she expected to be a night she'd always remember. Subdued lighting only enhanced the candlelight at each table. Rich, earth-toned shades of green, amber, and burgundy covered the chairs, booths, and walls. The ebony-colored wood floor beneath her feet added to the elegance of the setting. Tall windows boasted a view of the mountains.

A man in a dark suit standing behind a podium greeted her.

"Holly Harris, here to meet Matthew Cooper."

"Yes, miss. Mr. Cooper hasn't arrived, but the other two in your party have."

"Excuse me?" She turned to where he gestured. Matt's sister, her possible future sister-in-law Cathy, sat beside her boyfriend Pete in a booth against the side wall. The evening's expectations flew out one of those expansive windows. Swallowing hard, she made her way to the table and slid into the bench facing the other couple.

Cathy leaned forward. "Do you know what Matt's news is?"

"News? He asked me to dinner and told me to wear a little black dress." He and his sister were close. Did anyone propose with their sibling along for the ride? She didn't think so but allowed a little hope to leak back in.

"Me too. I had to borrow one. Pete insists a lawyer wears suits to work every day, even in casual Alaska, so he had plenty of formal clothes to choose from." She gave her significant other a loving expression.

Holly took a sip from the water glass already on the table. "I had to borrow a dress too."

"Jemma's closet?"

Holly blinked. "Yes, but how did you know?"

"Her special dresses are legendary. She could probably rent them out."

Holly chuckled. "I'll let her know. She's already an entrepreneur, so Jemma's Closet could be a new part of her business."

Cathy nodded enthusiastically.

"Um, did Matt give any hints about why we're here?" Brothers and sisters talked about things, right?

Pete spoke up. "I asked her the same question. Matt just said to meet him here."

Okay, sisters talked to each other, but everything she'd learned lately said brothers and sisters did not.

Cathy said, "Matt's always played it close to his chest. He doesn't discuss a situation until he has every detail worked out. No one knew his choice of university until the acceptance letter arrived, including Mom and Dad. The same thing happened when he decided to become a police officer."

"I'd always assumed he'd wanted to be in law enforcement since he was a boy."

She shook her head. "Danger? Guns? Criminals? Not Matt. We thought he would be in retail management like me. Never, not once, did we think he'd be a cop. Then, one day, he told us he'd been accepted into the Alaska State Troopers."

As Holly began to wonder if he might indeed be ready to propose in front of his sister—wouldn't a man with such a history leave no clues?—the subject of their conversation walked toward them. He worked out to stay fit for his job, and those muscles showed even dressed in a suit.

As he took the seat beside her, she wished they'd been seated across from each other. Seeing his expressions might have helped her know the fate of the evening.

"I'm glad everyone could make it tonight." He gave Holly what seemed a meaningful glance, one she thought signaled happy things to come. But then he turned and gave his sister and her man the same look—at least as far as she could tell. Matt picked up the menu in front of him. "I've wanted to eat here for years. It's my treat. Appetizers, anyone?"

The four of them agreed on two to share, Holly reserving space for the desserts she'd already checked out. A proposal would probably take away her appetite, but this felt less and less like a proposal or about anything of importance, and more like two couples sharing dinner. She'd dressed up, driven to Anchorage, and he was buying. So she would enjoy the meal.

Halfway through their entrees, Cathy said, "I can't stand it anymore. I have to tell." She gave Pete a meaningful glance.

He laughed, and a blush hit his cheeks. "Sure."

Cathy reached into her small, black evening bag—probably borrowed like Holly's—and came out with a ring. She slid it onto her left ring finger.

Matt's fork hit his plate. "My sister's getting married?"

Cathy sighed. Just as the woman earlier had, she turned her hand slowly from side to side to see the diamond in the light. "Yes."

"When is your wedding?" Holly asked.

"Wedding," Cathy said slowly, drawing out the word. "We both love the snow, so we've decided on January. We're going to be married in a small inn in Talkeetna. Just family and close friends. You're invited, of course, Holly."

Matt signaled their waiter. "This calls for champagne."

Holly stared down at her meal, wondering if it would be polite to continue eating the delicious seafood pasta dish, or if she should wait for the toast to the happy couple.

Cathy must have sensed her discomfort. "Everyone, please keep enjoying your meal. I've known about this for three days, so I'm over that initial can't-eat-a-thing sensation."

Pete turned to her with mock indignation. "Hey, you're not thrilled to be marrying me anymore?"

Cathy giggled and snuggled close to her intended. "Thrilled and planning to stay that way."

"I can't take much more of this." Matt stabbed a piece of his steak and brought it to his mouth. His grin told his sister he'd been teasing.

The waiter brought their champagne and served it in narrow flute glasses as Holly finished her shrimp scampi over linguine. After the man had whisked their plates away, he returned. "Dessert and champagne are made for each other." He listed their desserts, and Holly mentally chose hers halfway through.

She spoke up and ordered. "Fresh strawberry cheesecake." Cathy ordered the same, Pete chose a brownie with caramel sauce, and Matt the mocha-frosted chocolate cake.

Zero expectations of major news from Matt gave Holly a healthy appetite. She didn't want to analyze why not getting a proposal made her happier than getting one. A layer of fresh strawberries rested on top of cheesecake, with a strawberry sauce swirled through it. Her first bite made her as happy as she'd expected. As she brought a second forkful to her mouth, Matt tapped his glass.

"Everyone, I have some news of my own." He grinned like a boy and glanced her way.

Holly returned her fork to her plate and felt heat rise to her cheeks.

"A dream I've had for quite a while is coming true."

Sounded like a proposal to her. Fear tore through her.

"It's been a while in the making."

Holly gulped as he paused dramatically, and she prepared to extend her left hand for the ring.

"I've accepted a new position with the troopers."

Cathy said what Holly thought. "A promotion? You brought us here to tell us about a promotion?"

"Yes, I did. And the pay will be similar, but my duties will change. I'm going to be in the Bush more than out."

Cathy once again asked what Holly was thinking. "When will we see you?"

"There won't be a schedule that's regular."

A decided chill fell over the occasion.

Matt surveyed the quiet table. "I thought everyone would be happy for me."

Feeling dumbfounded, Holly found similar expressions on Cathy and Pete's faces.

"We'll miss you. That's all," Cathy said.

"Hey, it isn't like I'm moving to Antarctica. I'll be a short flight away. You can visit me anytime you want. And I'll be in town regularly, so we'll see each other then." He turned to Holly when he spoke his last words.

Did this mean they had a future? Or was this the big dump scene? "When are you moving?"

"I'll keep my house in the Valley, but I won't be living there full-time."

She dipped her head so she wouldn't have to look at him. What should she say at a moment like this? *Thank you for dumping me* after *dinner. I would have walked out if you'd done it earlier, and missed a lovely meal.*

Cathy's eyes darted from her brother to Holly. It seemed as though she wondered about their relationship, too. Holly had grown to think of Cathy Cooper as a friend, and at moments she'd assumed she'd become her sister-in-law some day in the not-too-distant future. When Cathy opened her mouth to say more, Holly gave a slight shake of her head.

Holly turned to Matt with a forced smile pasted on her lips. "We can talk about this after dinner—right, Matt?" Her gaze shifted to Cathy, and her friend gave a single nod that she understood Holly wanted to do this her way.

"Of course." Matt caught their waiter's attention and paid the check. With that done, he slid to the edge of his seat and stood. "We can all walk together to our cars."

Pete got to his feet, and Cathy followed him. "We'll head out on our own now. Pete and I need to rush to get somewhere else."

Her fiancé turned to her. "We do?" At Cathy's glare, he said, "Yes, I must have forgotten. Right, we have to leave." Holly hoped he didn't babble like this in front of a courtroom. Of course, he didn't have his bride-to-be glaring at him then.

The couple made a hasty exit, leaving Matt on his feet and Holly still seated. She slid over, stood and reached for her purse—a small silver one that Jemma said went with the sparkles on her shoes. Matt held his elbow out for her, and she slipped her hand through it, cringing a little at the intimacy this implied. Holly smiled and said the usual things to the host near the door as they exited the restaurant. They'd had a lovely meal. Yes, she would love to return. But she didn't speak to Matt.

Trying to find the right words to ask about their relationship's status, she rehearsed a few questions in her mind. *Will you be staying in a small bachelor apartment in the Bush? Or will you have room for visitors? Have you just broken up with me, but so badly that I can't tell?*

Until the restaurant's door closed behind them and she'd checked the area to be sure no one could overhear, she didn't say another word to him.

Matt must have waited for the same moment. "Can I call you when I'm in town?"

His words sounded more like those of a friend, and not a close friend. "What? Why would you ask that?"

She felt him shrug. "I have to leave for the Bush in the morning. I'll be away from this area more than I'll be here."

"I see. You don't want to date anymore?"

He stopped and faced her. "Holly, I'm not ready to have a family. I didn't pursue a deeper relationship with you once I'd done a background check on you and learned about your kids. I'm just not ready," he repeated.

Holly sucked in her breath. The trooper had run a check on her. He didn't even want to meet her girls, and she had two amazing kids. Sure, she shouldn't have hidden that fact, but this just increased her feeling that she'd been living a lie throughout their time dating.

"I know I should have told you about them."

"It wouldn't have mattered. I'm focused on my career. I protected you and kept our relationship on a platonic level."

"Uh huh. Matthew Cooper, friends don't usually kiss."

"Every once and a while, I'd forget. I apologize for that."

Now he was sorry he'd kissed her? Could this night sink any lower?

"But I do want us to stay friends. Now that everything is out in the open, we could get together when I'm in town."

Matt didn't want her because she had kids, but he wanted to be friends—probably friends with benefits.

He took a step closer. "I wondered if we could be more than friends."

"But not with any future beyond a few nights of fun."

The lusty expression on his face was one he'd never had before. She hadn't known this Matt at all. As a shriek built up in her, a man bundled up in his coat hurried by, reminding her of their very public location.

Holly pointed over her shoulder. "My car's there."

Matt stood taller and scanned the area, acting as the law enforcement officer he was. "I want to walk you to your car."

Holly spun on her heels and hurried the half a block to her car. Her feet reminded her that Jemma's borrowed high heels almost always hurt—Bree would concur—but she didn't slow down. The sooner she was in the car with the engine on, the sooner Matthew Cooper became her past instead of her present.

"Will I see you again?" Matt asked as she unlocked the door.

Was he kidding? "I can tell now that we never had a relationship. If we did, you would have discussed your new job, and the changes it would bring. And I would have told you about my kids." For this and many reasons—a list that grew longer by the second—she added, "I think it's best if we don't date—or do anything else." *Because I want to rip your eyes out*, she thoughtfully kept to herself. "I consider Cathy my friend, so our paths may cross in the future, but never romantically." She climbed inside and inserted the key in the ignition.

"Holly, I don't understand." He actually had a pleading tone in his voice. The man didn't have a clue about how much he'd hurt her. "I just don't want kids. You didn't tell me about them, so I didn't tell you I knew."

She turned the key in the ignition and flipped on the headlights. "My kids are the best things in my life; they're the best part of me." She slammed the door shut and hit the lock button for good measure. When she pulled out, she saw Matt standing at the curb for a few seconds. Then he spun on his heels and walked in the other direction.

Men could be so clueless. Her car's clock told her it was almost nine-thirty. She fumbled in her purse with her right hand and pulled her phone out, punching Bree's number. She and Michael lived just a few blocks away. She could use some emotional support before she tackled the hour drive down a dark highway toward home.

Bree picked up before the second ring. "Dr. Harris." She must have been on-call for one of her clients.

"Bree, if you're up . . ."

"We're up. Are you okay? Do you need for us to help you? We could be out the door in two minutes. Right, Michael?" she heard her say, away from the phone's speaker.

"Stay where you are, Bree. I need a sister's opinion right now. Michael can give a man's perspective."

"If you're all right, then he must have proposed!" Bree said gleefully.

"Not a chance. He's leaving town. See you in five." She hung up as she swung onto their street, then into the underground garage.

Holly paced from one side of Bree and Michael's living room to the other. Daylight at two hours shy of midnight still surprised her, even after four years in Alaska. The mountains framing Anchorage's eastern view remained clear. The state's beauty usually left her in awe. Tonight, the view didn't help. The caffeine in the cup of coffee Michael had handed her may not have helped her situation either.

"A proposal!" Holly shouted. She turned toward her sister and brother-in-law, seated side by side on the couch. They jumped at her mini-explosion. "He told me to dress up." She stabbed a finger at her chest and blew out an angry breath. "No one wears a little black dress so a boyfriend can say he's leaving town."

Bree cleared her throat. "Very true."

"Maybe you misread the signs?" Michael said.

Bree laughed. "Like men give off accurate signs."

Looking and sounding indignant, he said, "That isn't true. My signals must have been right. We're happily married."

She laughed again. "Sure. But we both got on a plane to leave the great state of Alaska. Our signals were messed up. If we hadn't been on the same plane . . ."

Michael put his arm around Bree and kissed her cheek. "You're right."

Holly's anger vanished with their show of affection. Good men did exist. Taking a step toward a chair, she realized her feet still suffered the fate of Jemma's shoes. She kicked them off and felt the soft carpet underfoot for a moment before she sank into the chair she knew would be equally comfortable.

"Am I a bad judge of men or just of my own emotions?" She sank into the chair's softness. "Matt found out about the girls anyway." A scholarly quote came to mind, making her think of English professor Adam: *Oh! what a tangled web we weave when first we practice to deceive.* "Even with this happening, never again will I tell a man that I have kids."

Bree leaned forward in big sister concerned mode. "Are you sure that's wise?"

At Holly's nod, Bree glanced at her husband.

Michael stepped in. "Holly, you *do* have kids. That's a fact we can't ignore."

Leave it to the software engineer to find a scrap of logic in her situation.

Her sister said, "Unless you plan to date a man for more than a decade before marrying him, Ivy and Abbie will be part of the picture." She paused. "You aren't considering sending them off to boarding school or something like that, are you?"

"No, I love my girls more than anything." Holly covered her face with her hands.

Bree and Michael spoke in whispers; then someone, maybe both of them, rose to their feet. Michael's voice faded as he said, "I'll leave you women to talk."

Bree set her hand on Holly's arm. "It's getting late."

Holly jumped to her feet. "I'm so sorry. I've kept you up past your bedtime." She felt her face color at what that now meant for Bree. "I'll call you tomorrow. But not early." Holly searched for her evening bag. She remembered dropping it somewhere when she'd entered their condo. Not on the dining room table. She hurried over to the kitchen island, leaning over the top of it. It wasn't in the kitchen.

"Nonsense. You aren't going anywhere tonight."

Holly stopped. "What?"

"There's a guest room waiting for you."

Holly waved the comment away. "No. Once I find my purse . . ." Where was it?

Bree put an arm around her shoulder and led her down the hall. "You're too rattled to drive an hour. I prescribe a night in this comfortable bed. Guests say it's heavenly."

Their queen-sized guest room bed drew her in—an oasis of fluffy blankets and a down comforter, with calming decor. "Jemma did a wonderful job decorating this room."

"Yes, she did."

Bree pointed through an open door across the room. "Towels and toiletries, toothbrush, toothpaste, etc., are in the attached bathroom. Your favorite scent—a special strawberry body wash—is in the shower." Gesturing to the tall dresser to their right, she said, "There are a T-shirt and shorts with a robe in the top drawer. I'll see you in the morning."

Her sister exited, closing the door.

Over at the dresser, she tugged open the drawer and pulled out the clothing. When she'd changed and taken a hot shower, she felt like some of the day had been washed away.

The room felt perfect—too perfect to be coincidental. Her favorite scent of body wash. The kind of PJs she preferred. Her missing purse now sat on the dresser. Michael! He'd left the room and set all this up. Her sister had married a great guy. Both of her sisters had. They would tell her that the right guy was out there, waiting for her.

Settling under the cozy down comforter, her stress level dropped a fraction. When she reached for her phone and pulled up the last group of photos her mother had sent—some of the girls out on Lake Louise—it dropped more. Abbie and Ivy would be back in her arms soon. She flipped too far back, and the photo Jemma had taken not many hours before slid onto the screen. Her *pre-engagement* photo.

Holly closed her eyes, praying that the saying about everything looking better in the morning would be true.

She'd been dumped. Holly opened her eyes and stared at the soft, sky blue of the ceiling. Sitting up, she slid her feet into the slippers her host had placed beside the bed. If Bree ever tired of being a doctor, she'd need to contact Michael's sister Leah and her husband-to-be Ben to see if they needed help at their bed and breakfast.

A shower would wake her up—and Bree had been accurate in knowing Holly would relish every moment with the strawberry shower gel. In a hotter-than-hot shower, the best kind for waking up, she lathered up her hair with shampoo from a tiny hotel bottle. Bree had stayed in hotels on every trip she and Michael had taken to New York City, so she must have a huge stash of them somewhere. Following that with the conditioner beside it, she considered how she'd gone wrong.

Matt had given every sign of a future. Of course, that had been before he'd learned about the girls. He'd been busy at work, so she'd credited that to his less ardent kisses. Still, he'd kept calling, texting, dating her. He must have enjoyed her company. Just not the fact that she had two girls.

The cutest, sweetest kids ever to be on this planet.

Holly finished her shower and toweled off before stepping back into the slippers and robe Bree had loaned her. She knew Matt had emotionally walked away from their relationship months ago. The saddest part wasn't that; it was the fact that she'd thought a relationship beyond friendship existed. She felt like a pathetic creature. How could she have dreamed of marrying a man who not only didn't love her but didn't even want to have a close relationship with her?

Bree would tell her to take a deep breath and calm down. Jemma would make a bagel for her.

Both might help. Stepping back into the bedroom, the scent of breakfast wafted in. It smelled like pancakes or waffles she could slather with syrup, but she knew better.

Bree's breakfasts leaned toward super healthy and sometimes tasted a bit too much like twigs. Once she'd eaten whatever it was, she could go home and de-stress.

Chapter Eleven

After a peanut butter and jelly sandwich for lunch with Ivy's favorite, her homemade strawberry jam, Holly sat in front of her laptop. This morning, she simply hadn't cared about work or much of anything.

Her wallet cried out now that she hadn't taken Adam house hunting either the day before or today, but the anticipation of yesterday's dinner had consumed her, and she'd pushed him off until Thursday. She did look forward to working with him, though, and that surprised her. The Dr. O'Connell she'd watched from her seat in class didn't seem at all like this fun, interesting, more-than-a-little-bit-sexy man.

Scrolling through the agent's only site, she searched for houses for a different client—a family moving to Alaska this fall—and emailed the selections to them. Then she set up some viewings for a woman who hadn't decided if she wanted to buy a house or not. Holly suspected that she wouldn't buy one anytime soon, but she'd been booked for a week for all-day Wednesday.

With business taken care of, she shifted to a personal matter she didn't want to put off a second longer. Looking back, she wasn't sure why she'd considered a long-term relationship with Trooper Cooper, but she had. A stack of wedding magazines said so. And bridal sites online could be addictive.

Without checking what they held, she deleted the folder labeled "wedding," then the one labeled "stepchildren"— research about integrating her girls into a new marriage. She'd never liked the term stepchild anyway. It somehow sounded less than just *child*.

Staring at the slightly reduced list of folders, she said, "Pathetic. Holly Harris, you are pathetic." She paused for a moment. "No, you *were* pathetic. You aren't going to be stupid like this again."

Her former favorite folder, from the time before her wedding obsession, called to her. Its simple label of "pies" didn't even begin to reveal its importance. Opening the folder, she clicked on a recipe for coconut-chocolate pie. The two flavors had been a favorite combination of hers since her first childhood bite of a famous candy bar filled with one and coated with the other. Of course, hers would be the dark chocolate version. She'd been a discriminating child. Or picky.

Scanning through the list of ingredients, she saw that she did have everything. Pulling ingredients out of the cupboards and fridge, she began her work. Would Matt have liked this dessert? She wasn't sure. She must not have known him as well as she'd thought.

As Holly began measuring and putting ingredients in a bowl for the crust, she decided to double the recipe. If one pie de-stressed, two had to be better. This was a two-pie day if she'd ever had one.

While mixing, then forming the crusts, she ran through what she had on hand for the second pie. Not enough milk for a second pudding-type pie, and not enough apples for an apple pie.

She stopped work for a minute and went through her fridge and cupboards. A few apples and a can of cherry pie filling would be yummy together. Topping it with a brown sugar crumb mixture would be easy.

Holly slid one crust into the oven. Then she got to work on the fruit pie's filling, adding a generous dash of cinnamon and some nutmeg for fun. After removing the baked crust from the oven, she filled the unbaked pie shell with the apple and cherry mixture, added the topping, and put it into the oven. She cooked the chocolate filling for the creamy pie, cooled it over ice, then poured the mixture into the baked shell, and topped it with coconut before putting it into the fridge.

She washed up the dishes—her least favorite part of making pies—and she called the event a success. Her pie day had given her the peace she'd sought. Focusing on baking meant she couldn't think about last night. Just as she was about to sit down and relax, the timer went off for the fruit pie. Once it was out of the oven and on a cooling rack, she checked the time.

It was 2 p.m., and she had the rest of the day to herself. Little girls weren't playing nearby, making happy sounds, or even unhappy ones when a disagreement occurred. Having a sister outing was out. She knew Jemma would be busy on her projects. Bree had said she had to work today.

It looked like work was her best option. That, or writing— and how could she write about even a hint of romance the morning after being dumped?

Placing her laptop on the once-again-clean kitchen counter, she searched for properties for Dr. O'Connell. Big yard. Average or larger house. A woodsy feel. She watched a video, if there was one, and went through photos of the others. By the time she'd compiled a list of ten that fit his specs, she was starting to feel like writing. Maybe it *would* clear out the previous night's happenings if she gave her characters a happy dinner together, one that helped them on their way to love.

She dove into her story. As it started to flow, her phone rang. Debating for a few seconds whether or not she should answer, Holly decided to at least pick it up in case her girls needed her. The photo on the screen showed her writing nemesis, Dr. O'Connell, the last man she wanted to talk to when she felt confident about her story. Starting to set it down, she changed her mind. The man might have messed with her mind when it came to writing, but he could also pull her out of financial distress.

"Hello, Dr. O'Connell. I hope you're having a great day." A pause made her wonder if that was true.

"I am, but I wondered if my real estate agent would like to go out for a late lunch."

Her former professor and current client couldn't be interested in her as a woman, could he?

"So we can discuss the house hunt," he hurriedly added.

No. It wasn't her week for men. The fact that she might have welcomed his interest was a subject for another time. Or maybe one she didn't ever want to consider.

"I've already eaten lunch. Sorry."

"Well, could we go somewhere for dessert—a sweet treat and cup of coffee?"

The scents of her recent baking event still filled the house. Wondering if she'd regret what she was considering, she plowed ahead anyway. "Do you like pie?"

"Sure. Does a local place do pie well?"

"Yes. I enjoy baking and just made two. You can help me eat them if you'd like."

"Homemade pie? Are you kidding? I'm on my way. Could I stop and pick up coffee for us?"

He was considerate, she'd give him that. "I'd love that. Something simple for me, not sweet because of the pie. Just black with two creams."

"Consider it done."

She heard a bark on the other end. "You can bring Emma if you'd like."

"She'd love to come. Going for a ride and exploring a new place top her list for excitement. After eating, of course. Maybe she can have a piece of pie crust."

This friendly man couldn't be her former professor. "I'll text you my address."

She battled through the surge of panic that rose in her chest as she wrote the short text, wondering if she should tell him he couldn't come over after all. She'd just invited not only a client but her former, oh-so-stuffy professor into her home. Except he didn't seem very stuffy, maybe not stuffy at all, when he wasn't in class.

Deciding she had time to vacuum, Holly pulled it out, ran it over the floor, and shoved it back in the closet. Then she straightened the couch pillows and wondered if she should clean more. Her house was fine. No kids' toys littered the floor. No little fingerprints smeared the white-painted cupboards. She'd be glad when her girls came home.

Kids! Framed photos of her girls sat scattered about the living room. Precious pictures stored out of sight seemed wrong. Gathering them up, she pondered the wisdom of her actions. She realized that Dr. O'Connell wasn't part of her personal life; he was a client and nothing more. Not stopping to question the twinge of regret at that thought, she stowed the photos carefully in her bedroom closet.

Returning to the living room, she found it emotionally empty. Maybe she should adopt a new policy of telling everyone she had kids. The situation with Matt plowed into her. Nope, she'd stay silent.

Holly stood at the window, watching for Dr. O'Connell. Then, realizing how ridiculous that would appear, she went back to her computer and switched from her novel to the real estate site so she could refresh her mind on his options.

The roar of a motorcycle followed by silence told her he'd arrived. Making her way to the door, she put on her professional demeanor. She was his real estate agent, not his friend—and certainly not anything more than that even though she'd had a momentary slip and invited him here. *Think professional.* She squared her shoulders and pulled open the door, finding him almost to her.

"Holly, I've come prepared." He held up a beverage carrier in one hand and two forks in the other, a dog leash around his right wrist. "I wanted to make sure there weren't any obstacles to the pie."

How could she be professional now? Giving in to his playfulness, she laughed. "I like a man who's ready for anything." Stepping back, she motioned him and Emma into her small house.

Adam stepped over the threshold and into a place he was surprised to find himself standing in. Holly's house. A small—tiny, really—living area with a vintage couch, chair, end tables, and lamps swept into a kitchen that held the basics and a decent-sized granite-topped peninsula with bar stools. He unclipped Emma's leash and let her explore.

"You've devoted a large percentage of this room to the kitchen."

Holly touched the countertop with nothing less than love. "Yes." She sighed. "Great-aunt Grace did some updates especially for me."

"Great-aunt?"

"She'd rented this house in the past, but let me live here for free so I'd be able to finish my degree more easily. That's why I moved to Alaska. When she died, she gave it to me in her will. She left Jemma her own home—the larger house—so she moved here, too."

One sister had scored the big house, the other a tiny one? Choosing his words carefully, he asked, "Do you wish you lived in the larger house?"

"Meaning aren't I upset that I, who already lived in Palmer, lost out on the big house to a sister who didn't?"

He took a step back. The smile on her face appeared genuine. "Yes, but I wouldn't have put it that bluntly."

"I love my little house. It's been a happy place for . . . me." Her hesitation seemed odd to him as if she'd almost said something else—"us," perhaps. Had Holly lived with a significant other? If so, he hadn't left any signs behind. Adam would have to figure out how he felt about her having that sort of past if and when he learned that truth.

Emma explored beneath the end table, backing out from under it with one of those stretchy things women used to pull their hair back—a bright-pink one—hanging from her mouth. It gave him the opportunity to inquire about a man. "Your house appears thoroughly girly."

"Jemma's touch. That's what I asked for. It's a very female house." She hesitated again, then shrugged before reaching into a cupboard and grabbing two small plates. "I made coconut-chocolate and apple-cherry. Which would you like?"

Caution reigned as he stepped around the corner to see if they had the appearance of a cook's first and second homemade pies. The fruit pie had a golden topping, the crust an even color. The chocolate pie was sprinkled with coconut. Holly knew her way around a kitchen. "Is a choice required? What if I want to try both?"

Holly put one of the small plates back into the cupboard and brought down a slightly larger one, eyes sparkling. "Then I'm happy to accommodate you. Sometimes I don't know what to do with the leftovers." She cut the slices, placed them on the plate, and handed it to him.

"Sometimes? Do you bake a lot of pies?"

She sighed again, this time not quite as happily. "Only when I'm stressed." Stepping back, she said, "I shouldn't have said that. You're a client. Clients shouldn't know about stress."

He took a bite of the fruit pie. The crust crumbled in his mouth, the fruity interior's slight cinnamon taste playing to his love of the spice. "I think that if the client isn't the cause of the stress, sharing is okay. Can I assume I'm not?"

Her grin stretched ear to ear. "Yes, Dr. O'Connell. In this case, you're not the cause of the stress." She paused. "Well, maybe a teeny bit of it."

He laughed. "I can live with that. Please, call me Adam."

Her mind appeared to whirl as she prepared arguments against that. A woman who kept a man in the role of professor would probably not accept a date.

He jumped into the pause. "I am no longer your professor." He tried the chocolate pie, the rich creaminess melting over his tongue with a chewy bite of coconut. As soon as he'd swallowed the first bite, he took another.

She nodded. "True."

After swallowing the second bite, he offered his next piece of logic. "I'd place you at about twenty-five? I'm only a few years older than you."

"Twenty-six."

"Even less than I expected. I'm thirty-one." He broke off a piece of the fruit pie's crust and leaned over to give it to Emma who sat still, right next to him, waiting for that to happen.

"Dr. O'Connell, I keep picturing you standing in the front of the classroom while I'm seated watching you teach. How would you have felt if I'd called you Adam then?"

"Right now, I'm sitting in your house. Eating the most amazing pie I've ever tasted."

His dog gave a single bark.

"See? Emma likes it too, and she's a baked goods connoisseur."

The grin reappeared. "It's good?"

He eyed what remained of his two slices. "My problem is deciding which one to take a bite of next."

"Excellent." She leaned her elbows on the counter and observed him. As she pondered, he finished up the apple-cherry pie and put his fork into the chocolate to work on it. "I'm happy you're enjoying the pies. Adam."

At her use of his first name, his fork skidded on the plate, and his fingers slipped into the chocolate pie.

When he held up his hand, she laughed. "I'll get you a wet towel to wipe it off."

"I'm fine." He licked the chocolate off his fingers one by one. "You do know that once you've watched a man lick dessert off his hand, you're permanently on a first-name basis."

She laughed again. "Whenever I'm tempted to call you Dr. O'Connell, I'll picture you with chocolate fingers."

"That sounds reasonable," he said as he licked the last bit of chocolate off his pinkie finger. Then he polished off his pie.

"More?"

He put his hand over his stomach. "I'd better not. As it is, that was lunch. I'd better leave room for a real, unsweetened dinner."

She took the plate from him and washed it at the sink. Her kitchen might be small, but it was tidy.

He walked over to the kitchen side of the counter, resting his hands on the flat surface as he observed her. "Need any help?"

"No. I don't like to let dishes pile up. When you don't have a dishwasher, they can get away from you pretty quickly."

He held up his hands. "I've got sticky fingers. Mind if I wash them in the bathroom while you're doing that?"

"Go ahead." She pointed down the hallway. "First door on the right."

Half a dozen steps took him to the compact home's hall. Family photos lined one side. Kids. Her sisters. Each of them with those kids. One with the kids and an older man. And one with kids and an older couple. The woman in the photo bore a striking resemblance to Holly, so those must be her parents. He wasn't sure whose kids they were, but someone in the family must claim them. Maybe a cousin who visited often.

A photo at the end of the line showed Holly and Matt, but no kids. His jealousy spiked, but he comforted himself with the thought that she didn't wear the man's ring—even after the big event last night. And she'd baked pies to de-stress, so maybe they'd parted ways. He'd never want anything bad to happen to Holly, but having the trooper out of the picture wouldn't upset him.

His next surprise came when he walked into the littlest room in the house and found a shower curtain covered in yellow rubber ducks. Cute, but hardly what an adult would choose. Washing his hands, he tried to come up with any reason a grown woman would have that. She'd been a student on a budget, so someone had probably given it to her when their kids outgrew the fun. He realized he preferred rubber duckies to the rose-covered shower curtain his mother had hung over the tub in her guest bathroom. He loved his mother, but her taste in decorating and his didn't intersect very often.

He washed his hands and walked back out, stopping at the end of the hall and leaning against the corner where it met the living area. Emma ambled over and sat on his foot. "Nice shower curtain," he said to Holly.

Holly's eyes widened, and she swallowed. "It's, uh, cute, isn't it?"

"Adorable," he said, the one word dripping with sarcasm. "And I liked the photo of you and the trooper. He'll be sorry he missed your pie."

Holly tensed. "He's . . . in the Bush. Well, I found some promising properties for you online." Her words tumbled out, one rushing into the next. "Would you like to see them on the screen before we go in person?" She tried to smile and failed, her mouth falling back into a neutral position.

Something he'd said had made her nervous. Maybe he shouldn't have commented on the photo. He felt like grinning over the fact that Matt wasn't around, but also like a jerk for upsetting her. Or, did she think he'd taken a jab at her tastes? "Holly, I like the shower curtain."

Her eyebrows shot up. "You do?!"

"Like might be too strong of a word. But it isn't a problem for me, and so much nicer than pink roses on white—roses that match embroidery on the towels."

Holly stared at him.

"All true." When she gave him a puzzled frown, he added, "Not my home. My parents'."

"Okay. I thought that sounded *very* strange for a bachelor."

"My mother's design choices. That shower curtain hangs above the bathtub I use when I visit. Rubber duckies trump pink roses every time."

She grinned. "Then thank you for the backward compliment."

"My pie compliment is that they're straight-up awesome. In fact, Mom would want both of those recipes. Dad loves chocolate and cherries, so they'd be winners."

"I made up one on the fly, but I can send you a link to the chocolate pie. I found it online."

Those pies, still resting on the counter, called to him. "Would you mind giving me a piece of each to go? Your pie might be better than my mom's. But don't tell her that."

Adam thought she'd smiled before, but now she seemed lit from within. He realized he'd never seen her smile that way when she'd been his student. If compliments made her react like this, but she'd always seemed stressed out in his class, he wondered where he'd gone wrong with his teaching.

How did you ask that question? *Gee, it seems I might not have been the greatest teacher—can you criticize me? Oh, and I'll still buy a house from you, don't worry.* That would be a conversation that would need to wait until they knew each other better. Much better.

He scooped Emma up and sat on the couch, settling her on his lap.

The silence made him look up to find her watching him. The moment stretched to the point of being uncomfortable when Holly pulled her eyes away and pointed to the open laptop at the side of the counter. "I went through dozens of properties to whittle them down to these ten. I hope there's a winner in here."

He motioned her over to where he sat. "We can look here."

"No!" she almost shouted. "Sorry. That couch is showing its age and is a little soft. People who sit side by side almost sink into the same hole." She shrugged. "Jemma may be a wonderful decorator, but she had to work with what I had."

"Then?"

"We can sit on bar stools at the counter. That's where I work."

"I'm happy to do that." Adam set his dog on the floor and returned to his stool at the counter. He tugged the computer toward himself to look at her options.

Holly pulled out a plastic container and lifted a slice from both pies into it. "I'm going to take the rest of these pies to Jemma's. If I leave them here, I'll eat them. The three of you can have pie tomorrow."

"For breakfast?" he asked hopefully.

"I'm pretty sure some will be left. Maybe warm the fruit pie in the microwave to make it seem more like a real breakfast."

"Any plan that makes pie into a real meal is one I can support." He checked out the property on the computer screen as Holly wrapped the pie pans and put them in the fridge. Trees surrounded the house, so this real estate agent had taken instruction better than Dennis.

Not wanting to click anything on that page that might mess her up, his eyes moved to the top of the screen. A word processing window sat open. Would this give him insight into Holly? Feeling like he was invading her privacy, but curious, he glanced over at his host and saw her fishing around in a cupboard—probably for the elusive lid to the container she'd used for his pie. He clicked on the window, and the page in front of him filled with text. Scanning it, he realized it was fiction, a short story, or maybe even a book manuscript.

"Hey, that's personal!" Holly said from next to him. She reached over and clicked back to the real estate site. The happy person he'd seen not long ago had vanished. Next to him stood a woman with tears simmering in her eyes.

Guilt sank into him. He *had* invaded her privacy. "I'm sorry. It was open. I was bored. I didn't think it through."

She rested her face in her hands.

He stood. "Maybe I should go."

"No. You're fine. It's me."

"How can this be about you when I went where I shouldn't have?"

She straightened and looked heavenward for a moment, then at him. "The problem is that I want to be a writer—that's a book, if you didn't have enough time to figure it out. But you always made it clear, abundantly clear, in class that I don't have the talent."

The hurting woman in front of him didn't resemble the woman from moments ago. "Why do you think that? You were an excellent student."

"Right." She rolled her eyes. "That's why you shredded everything I wrote. I worked as hard as I could, but you never said I did a decent job. I've graduated, so you don't need to be kind to me. You splashed your thoughts about my writing abilities across every assignment with red ink. A lot of red ink. I just haven't been able to let go of my dream."

He sat down, landing hard on the stool. "You were the best student I'd had. I wanted to push you, to help you excel as a writer."

She tentatively spoke. "You *liked* my writing?"

He nodded. "I failed as a teacher. I failed you." Here he'd thought teaching suited him, yet he'd torn down his best student. How had the others felt? Had each of his students walked out of his classroom feeling incompetent? He might have to email every one of his top students to reassure them. He didn't want to redirect lives based on wrong input.

"I can write? I mean, I know I *can* write—but I write well? Being an author isn't a stupid dream?"

"Yes, you write well. It isn't a stupid dream." His opinion of his teaching abilities dropped another notch. He'd stomped all over her dreams.

"Yes!" Holly shook her fists in the air. She reached over and brought her book back up on the computer screen. "Is this any good?"

"Do you really want *me* to weigh in on your writing?"

After pondering that for a moment, she said, "As crazy as it might sound, I trust your abilities as a teacher. It's hard for me to admit it to myself, but I grew in leaps and bounds when I was your student. Now that I know you liked what I wrote, your opinion will hit me differently. More like a gentle breeze instead of a hurricane."

What he'd seen did need work; first drafts always did. But she had the talent, and it could be a great book. "Is the whole book finished?"

She held her thumb and forefinger an inch apart. "So close I can taste it. I think I can finish it in a week. Maybe less." She swirled in a circle. "Maybe a lot less, now that I know I can write. Whew! That's taken a load off me." Before he knew what was happening, Holly's arms reached around him and pulled him into a hug. He wrapped his arms around her waist and felt her warmth sinking into him. Then, just as suddenly as she'd hugged him, she leaped backward.

"I'm so sorry." Her hands went to her cheeks, now stained pink. "You're my client, my former professor. We *don't* have a personal relationship. Now you can see what happens when I call you by your first name."

Adam carefully weighed his words, wanting to be honest but not scare her off. "Holly, if that's the result of using my first name, feel free to call me Adam anytime you want." He stood. Leaving now, before things turned more awkward, felt like the right thing to do. He started for the door. "I appreciate the awesome pie. I need to drop Emma off and run a few errands."

"Should I schedule appointments to see these houses Thursday?" She sounded tentative, as though she still didn't believe he wanted to work with her.

"Please. Anytime is fine." He reattached his dog's leash. "Ready for a ride, Emma?"

She barked, and he heard Holly laugh. "I'll pick you up about ten, day after tomorrow, okay?"

An idea popped into his mind. "Will we still be out at lunch time?"

"Oh yeah."

"Then I'm taking us to lunch." Emma barked again. Looking down at his furry friend, he said, "Not you. You get to spend the day in Jemma's backyard. Maybe your new friend Chloe will come to visit, and you can have lunch together." Standing straight again, he found Holly staring at him with a confused expression on her face. Confusion probably worked in his favor. At least, he hoped it did.

After Adam's visit and the embarrassing hug incident, Holly wanted to either crawl under a rock or read. She decided to go with the latter. She walked down the hall, heading toward the book's current home, the nightstand beside her bed. As she did, it seemed like the left wall flashed with neon lights. She'd forgotten about the family photos lining it.

He knew about her girls. Why hadn't he asked about them? Something like, "Hey, it's obvious you have kids." As she studied them, she realized that Abbie and Ivy were in most of them, but they weren't just with her. They were with her parents, her sisters—one even had them with their great-uncle, her dad's brother who'd visited them a couple of years ago.

Maybe he didn't know they were hers. Keeping her kids out of her romantic life was the only answer she saw. When Matt had found out on his own, he'd pulled back emotionally and eventually ended the relationship. But, more important than her feelings, she knew the only way to protect her girls emotionally was to make sure her dating life did not intersect her family life. Too bad that romantic life was now non-existent.

Matt was a nice guy, but one of his main selling points had been that she'd thought he'd be a good dad for her girls. She needed a great husband *and* a great father for them. A breath of fresh air swept through her. She wouldn't choose a man just for her girls. She had to love him, at least a little.

Then she'd tell this future mystery man about the girls.

Continuing to her bedroom, she thought of the warmth of Adam's arms wrapped around her, and she wondered if not having a man in her life was completely true. This man didn't scream husband or father material. But having his arms around her had made her heart flutter more than a little.

Book in hand, she returned to the living area, ready to sink into a story for an hour. Spotting her computer, she knew work had to come first. She set the book down and patted it fondly. "I'll be back to you soon." The luxury of reading in the middle of the day would be waiting for her.

She set up viewings for the ten houses she'd show Adam on Thursday. Surely one of those would be his dream house.

Chapter Twelve

House number thirty-four came onto the horizon. It was their third house of this day, part of what had become an almost a two-week house hunt. She hadn't realized Adam had been keeping track of the count too.

Until yesterday.

He'd stepped out of the car and stared at what had appeared to be a winner online. *"Thirty-one.* I'm not a believer in luck, but that's the same number as my age. It would be fun if this were the one for me." When he'd shaken his head at his first glimpse of the backyard, she knew it wouldn't work. Within three minutes, they'd been back in her car.

They'd begun house hunting by meeting each other at the address. They'd given up on separate vehicles a week ago. When they'd stayed out through the lunch hour, he'd insisted on taking her out and paying. He'd been nice through it all.

She was nowhere in the range of closing the deal on a house he wanted. Oh, she knew how to describe that perfect abode; she just hadn't discovered a match on the market. And she'd suggested again that he might want to build so he could have exactly what he wanted. He'd told her he didn't want to wait a year to move in. At this rate, it might take longer to find an already existing home.

Everything he said about the properties made sense, but she needed to sell him a house and soon. During one of their calls, her girls had asked when they'd be able to shop for school clothes. The idea of starting kindergarten excited them, and they'd always been girls who liked to dress up.

Their grandmother and great-grandmother had bought them several new outfits, but they needed more. And they'd also managed to outgrow their winter coats from last year. She'd have to hit thrift shops when she had a chance. Her girls grew so quickly that she needed options.

As she and the man she'd come to think of as Adam, no longer Dr. O'Connell, had searched for his dream home, one thing stood out: the land was more important than the structure. His vision for the house was easy. He wanted a three-bedroom, two-bathroom house with a two-car garage. The land it was sitting on had become the sticking point. Just as she'd thought she understood and could find him something in the more rural areas beyond Wasilla, he'd said he didn't want to drive that far once winter came.

Again, a valid point, but not getting her closer to a sale.

She'd managed to maintain a professional distance between them, even though Adam had been more and more personable. Once, she'd told him the opening with a railing that overlooked a home's living room was known as a Juliet balcony. He'd stepped up to it and dramatically recited the famous balcony scene from Shakespeare's play.

He'd made her laugh that day and every other day. Except for today. On this sunny and otherwise nice day in July, Adam was cranky.

Her client spoke from the passenger seat. "I like the front of this listing." That sounded promising. He turned to check out the neighborhood through the side window. "I hope the backyard measures up to the online photos."

"Me too." She stopped the car and put it in park. "The interior is easy to see in the online photos. I could tell that the kitchen, dining room, and living room had potential. The outside appeared okay, but sometimes the exterior photos have been—"

"Misleading." Adam popped open his door.

"Not the word I would have chosen, but there's some truth in what you said. Photographers use the angle that makes a property look its best."

"That's a nice way to say they lure you out to the property under false pretenses and hope you decide to buy it anyway." He closed the door, clearly tired of the search.

Holly sighed and followed his lead. One more reason she had to hurry and find him a place. Before he decided to try a third real estate agent.

He stood beside the house's front door, appearing none-too-happy about the upcoming experience. Would anything inside look right to a man in that state of mind?

"Adam, we can cut today's search short. Try again tomorrow."

Closing his eyes, he leaned against the side of the house. "I'm sorry, Holly. Looking at house after house and not finding what I want is disheartening." He straightened. "Let's keep going."

She unlocked the box hanging from the doorknob and took out the key, inserting it into the lock. When she pushed open the door, she stepped back to allow him to enter first, something she always did for her clients. Right inside the door lay the living room and dining area, with the kitchen peering out from around the corner.

Adam walked through to the kitchen, more quickly than he had in the other two houses that morning. He spent about a minute there, then went to the doors leading outside. She followed him onto a concrete patio, realizing they'd be moving on to house number thirty-five in a second or two.

"I can see the neighbor behind here."

She nodded. That had been a deal-breaker every time. Maybe she needed to preview each house. She'd done that with a few, but the distance between houses meant she could easily spend an entire day checking them out.

He spun on his heels and headed for the front door. She hoped he didn't jump ship and find another real estate agent. As Holly pulled the sliding glass door closed behind them and flipped the lock on it, she tried to find the right words to calm him down. There *would* be the right house for him. She just needed to convince him of that.

Adam's phone rang. He still looked grouchy as he took the device out of his pocket and glanced at the screen, stepping away from her as soon as he did. She heard "Yes, Dennis," then a pause. He went around the corner into the kitchen. She heard enough of Adam's muttered words to know he had replied. The name "Dennis" seemed familiar, like he'd mentioned it since she'd met him.

Not a brother's name. Adam hadn't ever said his brothers' names, or his father's. He had lived with a fellow professor—

Tim. So who . . . she whirled back toward the kitchen. His real estate agent. He'd given the man's name at some point. She'd never met a Dennis, so it stood out.

Not again! Not when she had invested so much time into her client. She must have used a couple of tanks of gas on the showings, plus the emotional wear and tear. She'd spent hours online searching for properties, calling listing agents, visiting properties in advance. This couldn't be happening. Only a slimy reptile would go back to his earlier agent after all her work. Hadn't he only this morning given her words of praise? If he looked happy after speaking with Dennis, she'd know the truth.

Adam rounded the corner, smiling widely. The lizard slid the phone back into his pocket.

Holly shifted from foot to foot. "Everything all right?"

"Fine."

Ask about the call, or be professional?

"Let's go to the next house."

Professional won.

They were soon back on the road, driving toward a house she wasn't sure he'd like due to distance.

"Holly, we've been driving quite a while. I'm starting to learn my way around the Valley, so I think we're beyond Wasilla, aren't we?" He scanned the land around them.

She chewed her lip. "Yes, the house is north of Wasilla, but wooded and with lake access."

As she slowed to make the turn off the highway, Adam checked his watch. "This is too far. It might be stunning, but I can't see myself driving ninety minutes to work every day. I guess it's the Juneau boy in me. Everything was close. After that, I lived on campus in college or a short walk from there."

She swung the car around and headed south, noting at the same time that she'd need to get gas in the near future. "I knew it was a long shot, but I was getting desperate." When he glanced at her with eyebrows raised in surprise, she slapped her hand over her mouth. "I'm so sorry. I hadn't realized I'd spoken those words out loud."

His slow, sexy smile appeared. "Have I been a challenge?"

"That sounds negative. You know what you want, and we haven't found it yet." Had his former agent come through? That elephant sat in the back seat.

They rode in silence, the minutes seeming to stretch into hours, every second growing more and more uncomfortable. Adam finally ended it. "Holly, we need to take a break. We've searched every day, and I feel like we're missing something."

Here it comes. He's about to tell me Dennis found the perfect place.

"I need to relax and regroup."

She'd have to borrow some money from Bree and Michael. Sure, it wasn't the end of the world, but a twenty-six-year-old woman with two kids entering kindergarten should have her act together. Shouldn't she?

"I clear my head when I fly."

If she had her sister and brother-in-law write a contract and charge interest, it would seem less like she'd failed.

"Seeing the world from above gives me a different perspective on the world below."

While Adam flew, she'd take a long walk—maybe go hiking to clear her head, then consider a second job for the summer.

"Let's keep driving to Merrill Field in Anchorage. I can take you up in my plane."

Maybe she could tutor kids over summer vacation. She did have a degree in education, after all.

"Holly? Are you listening?"

A gas station came into view, so she put on her signal and pulled up to the pump. "I heard you say you needed to find a new real estate agent, and that you liked flying." She reached for the door handle, but he put his hand on her right arm.

"Holly, I didn't say either of those things. I said that flying cleared my head and asked if you'd like to go up with me."

She blinked. She'd heard his words, but maybe she'd changed the meaning of them. "You did say something about taking me up in your plane. You mean you want me to fly with you?"

He nodded.

"You aren't firing me as your agent and going back to Dennis?"

He reeled back. "Why . . . oh, the phone call. You have an amazing memory if you remember me mentioning him once or twice. Dennis still didn't understand. He'd found another house in a regular subdivision."

"But you were smiling when you walked away."

"Yes, because I told him my real estate agent knew what I wanted and would find it."

Holly felt like a beam of light from heaven came down and touched her. "Your trust in me will be rewarded. I know what you want."

"It's just that it doesn't seem to be on the market, right?"

She nodded. "Right. I've even started searching for-sale-by-owner houses to see if I can find it."

He popped open his car door. "Let me do the macho thing and fill up your tank." He started to step out. "And then you'll fly with me?"

"I'd love to!"

Satisfied, he closed the door and whistled as he walked to the pump.

Holly relaxed and put her hand to her chest. None of her other clients were anywhere near a sale. But she still had him as a client and the hope of closing with him. There had to be a house out there for Adam O'Connell.

An hour later, Holly swung into Merrill Field, making turns as Adam instructed. She finally came to a stop next to an airplane, what Adam called his "tie-down." Living in Alaska meant that she knew there were many planes. They occasionally flew overhead in the most off-the-beaten-track places, but no one in her family or circle of friends flew. She'd never even been near a plane as small as the one Adam proudly stood next to.

"Here she is." He patted the wing. "Pretty, isn't she?"

Since she could honestly say she liked the pale-blue stripe on the white body of the plane, she agreed, but it just looked like a small airplane to her. "How many can fit in it?"

"A Cessna 172 seats four." He began checking out the plane.

That would work for the girls and us. Where had that thought come from? Abbie and Ivy would never be near this plane. Why would they?

She asked, "What are you doing?"

"Pre-flight. I'm making sure everything is as it should be. A safe pilot does a pre-flight every time."

Because he wants the airplane to stay in the air, she added his unspoken reason. As she watched him, her nerves started to jingle a bit. "You've been flying how long?"

"Ten years, give or take a few months."

"Any accidents?"

Adam paused and turned away from the plane to face her. "Are you nervous?"

She tried for a casual, relaxed shrug, but it felt edgy.

"Let me go back to where I should have started. Have you ever been in a small plane?"

"Never. I've noticed that they fall out of the sky quite a bit though."

He came toward her, placing his hand on her arm. Something about his touch calmed her. "I've never had the smallest bit of trouble with a plane. The weather is ideal for flying." He gestured to the blue sky with small puffy clouds overhead. "And I'm not planning to fly over wilderness or a mountain range today. We should be as safe as we were in the car coming here—the car, I might add, that you drove with no complaints from the passenger."

How did he manage to make her smile so easily? "Okay, I've decided to trust you. Let's be safe, but hurry so I can't change my mind."

"Will do." He gave her arm a small squeeze before releasing it, then returned to his check of the airplane. Probably ten minutes had passed when he said, "Climb on in. We're ready to roll."

Once seated in the plane with the door beside her snugly closed—she'd checked twice to be certain so she couldn't fall out—Adam startled her when he yelled "Clear" out his window. He started the plane, slipped a headset on, spoke into it, and they began moving forward at a slow but steady pace down the taxiway he'd pointed out earlier.

He paused the plane for a moment. "I'm about to pull onto the runway. You ready, Holly?"

She gulped and nodded. Holly Harris hadn't been afraid, at least not visibly, of much of anything else she'd had to do over the years. And there'd been some major challenges.

He spoke into his headset again, and they rolled forward with Adam taking them onto a different paved strip. He pushed levers, and the plane surged forward, moving faster and faster. Holly held onto the seat with both hands as they left land and floated skyward. Climbing upward, she began to wonder if they'd end up in the clouds by the time they leveled off.

Adam steered to the right, above the city. Then the solid ground dropped away, and they soared over mud and water—Cook Inlet at low tide. She'd only seen the edge of that body of water as she drove from Palmer to Anchorage and back. The view from above changed everything.

Lifting her head, she noticed for the first time that she was on even terrain with the mountains that defined the edge of Palmer and everything to Anchorage and beyond. Leaving water behind, the small plane flew over green forest snaked with rivers and dotted with lakes.

"How's your first flight?"

Her eyes flitted from one amazing sight to another. "It's the best! I never imagined how it would feel to do this."

"I know. Commercial airlines soar at high altitudes. There's a view, but . . ." His words drifted away.

"This is more intimate. I'm part of what I see. I feel like I could reach out and touch the water in that river."

Holly soaked up what would probably be her only flight in a small plane. She'd sell Adam his house and never see him again unless it was just in passing at the grocery store or somewhere like that if he bought a house near her.

"We could land on a strip and see a piece of this up close."

"No, I don't want to cut the flight short."

He made a slow turn to face the plane in the direction they'd come from. "Palmer's over there, isn't it?" Holly pointed to their left.

"Yes. Palmer's there, and Wasilla's a little more to the left."

Disappointment flooded her as they began crossing Cook Inlet again. "Are you going back so soon?"

"Not a chance when I have someone in my plane who enjoys this as much as I do."

Something beyond happy slipped inside her. She tried to push it out, but it wouldn't leave. She'd need to search for answers to the meaning later.

Adam angled the plane more toward Palmer. "I have an idea. When you pointed to Palmer, I wanted to see it from above. What if we flew that direction so I could get a better sense of the area?"

"Use flying as a real estate tool? I love that." She settled back in her seat and enjoyed the ride. When they reached land, they were above Birchwood and Chugiak. "Adam, you've been adamant about living in the Valley. As your real estate agent, I should point out that we're above an area you may want to consider. We're probably halfway between Palmer and Anchorage."

He glanced to his right. "Eagle River? No, thank you. I pulled off the highway to check it out a few weeks ago and found subdivisions that reminded me of Anchorage."

"Not Eagle River. Birchwood and Chugiak—especially Chugiak—for larger parcels of land." She pointed below them.

Adam put the plane in a slow turn. "I see a lot of trees."

"I should have mentioned it sooner. I'm sorry."

"No, it wouldn't have mattered. I would have told you I wasn't interested. But now that I'm above it, I can tell that this area hits many of my must-haves."

"It's also much closer to your job."

"One of my first thoughts was that it would be closer to Merrill Field. I want to be able to hop in my plane and go down to the Kenai to visit my parents, fish, explore the outdoors." He continued staring out his window. "There's a runway, a smaller one I'll grant you, but it's paved."

"Birchwood Airport. Would you like to have your plane near your house?"

"Are you kidding? That's fantasy land for a pilot. Yes!"

The circling motion started to make her spin. "Can we stop flying in a circle now?" She clamped her hands onto her head.

"Oh, sorry." He leveled them out. "Are you okay?"

Her equilibrium began to return. "Yes. But no more circles today, please."

"That's a deal. Let's head back." He steered the plane toward the big city on the horizon. As the tall city buildings grew larger, he added, "I'm excited about seeing some houses around here."

She hoped what he wanted existed there. The driving distance from some of the properties in the Valley had become one of her biggest hurdles. That was a non-issue in Birchwood and Chugiak.

Adam checked with the tower and brought them back to Merrill Field, reversing the process of their takeoff, this time with buildings moving by quickly as they approached land and touched down. After slowing the plane, Adam taxied them back to his plane's spot.

He turned off the engine, then walked around to help her down. As her feet touched the ground, Holly's knees folded up. Adam grabbed for her right arm, catching hold of it at the same moment she reached for a bar running from the wing to the body of the plane with her left. She preferred the touch of his hand for support. When she straightened, he let his arm drop.

Adam looked like a little boy who had been caught doing something he shouldn't have been. "Sorry about that spin. I think you're still feeling it."

She waved aside his comment. "I wouldn't change a second of that flight. I loved it! Thank you for a once-in-a-lifetime experience."

Adam stared at her for a second, as if he wanted to say something. Then, shaking his head slightly, he turned toward his plane and tied it back down with the ropes.

Back in her car, they returned to the Mat-Su Valley. Adam remained unusually quiet on the drive, but he leaned over in his seat to scan the area when they passed the sign for Chugiak. If she could find him a house this week, the deal would close in time for her to meet her little family's financial needs. And she'd see the last of her former professor. The odd thing was that the day before, that had felt like a better idea than it did now.

Chapter Thirteen

A dark-green door faced them from the end of the sidewalk. As they neared this first home of the day, their first in Chugiak, Adam could see that the green had been added over another color—probably decades ago. The paint had chipped off in random locations to reveal an earlier, unfortunate choice of orange.

Holly unlocked the door and pushed it open, stepping aside as she always did to allow him to enter first. Holly had been friendly and informal after their flight yesterday, but she was back in professional mode today.

He immediately noticed that large windows extended from the right of the door to the corner, making the street-facing side of the room feel bright and welcoming. A long wall to the door's left stretched to the back of the house, and wore 1970s era fake wood paneling.

Holly pointed at that wall. "The paneling appears to be original to the house. The good news is that you won't be paying for a renovation someone's already done that isn't to your taste. The bad news is that it might be pricey to fix everything."

A soaring cathedral ceiling with exposed beams lay overhead. "Now we're talking."

Holly's expression mirrored his own. "The photos showed an expansive great room, but I wondered if it was just skilled camera work in a tiny room. I had that happen once." She walked the perimeter of the room. "A dining table would fit well here." She stood outside an opening that gave a glimpse of a kitchen with a harvest-gold stove, worn vinyl floors, and faded Formica countertops.

He said, "I know vintage is in, but . . ."

"Worn out and vintage aren't necessarily the same thing. I understand. We can leave if there's no chance this will work. Don't feel like you have to look at the rest. I have more places scheduled for today."

Adam stepped over to a round, free-standing, black wood stove, a remnant of the 70s that he could enjoy. Standing there, the view out the set of sliding glass doors caught his eye. Woods extended into the distance; a mountain peered over the top.

"The land backs up to a state park. This house sits on 6.9 acres that no one can build behind."

Sliding the door open, he paused for a moment and took a deep breath of the clean, fresh air. A bird singing was the only sound. Stepping outside onto a large concrete patio, he noticed that a six-foot-tall wooden fence framed the yard. He could put Emma out there, and not worry about the little girl getting away.

He heard Holly step beside him. "Done."

"What do you mean?"

"Done. Sold. Where do I sign?"

She laughed. "I knew you'd like the backyard. Let's go see the rest of the house."

"I'm serious, Holly. I'm buying this house."

"Wait! Don't you want to see the rest of it? The master bedroom might have a closet-sized bathroom with a purple-tiled shower so tiny you can barely squeeze into it—or the bathroom door could slam the toilet every time you open it. I've seen both."

Adam took a deep breath. "You've shown me dozens of houses. I'd already seen a bunch in Anchorage." He pointed his thumb back at the house. "I can change that." Gesturing at the land around him, he added, "This is permanent."

She grabbed his arm. "Please. I need you to see the rest of the house before you sign."

"I don't need to."

"I need to be able to sleep at night knowing I sold you the house you wanted."

He turned to her, and something about the plaintive expression in her blue eyes made him stop and listen. He did enjoy her blue eyes, her face in general. Holly Harris' features and genuine personality charmed him, much like Romeo's interest in Juliet—but he hoped they'd have a happy ending.

"I'll do it for my real estate agent." As they went back inside, he added, "I can't envision a more perfect backyard. It reminds me of Nathaniel and Jemma's yard."

"See, it wasn't a waste of time to see those houses first."

Spending time with you would never be a waste of time, he thought, glancing over at her.

Holly dutifully led him upstairs and followed him in and out of the master bedroom with the same glorious view and an attached, but woefully outdated, bathroom. Both rooms turned out to be adequately sized. Two additional bedrooms came next, one with an odd loft to the side accessed by a ladder.

Holly said, "I can see kids having fun with that."

He didn't expect to have kids—especially kids old enough to climb a ladder—for years.

A hall bath, which needed a re-do as much as the master, and a bonus room large enough to be labeled a family room, completed the upstairs.

"All of the rooms are large or at least a decent size."

"I agree. I want to buy this house."

He hurried downstairs with Holly on his heels. The adrenaline of finding the right house—finally!—surged through him. Standing in the center of the great room with Holly beside him felt right. "We found it!" He picked her up in his arms and spun her in a circle. "Yes!" Setting her down, he stared into her befuddled face. Her expression didn't say "back off."

Her eyes moved to his lips, back to his eyes.

When he started to lean forward, she looked down at the floor. Stepping back, he wondered if he should have kissed her, if she would have kissed him back. *Slowly. Go slowly, O'Connell.*

"I think there's another room over there." Holly pointed to her right. The real estate agent had reappeared.

A small room almost behind the staircase must have been considered a bedroom at some point—it had a closet—but it was too small in his estimation. Enlarging the window to the backyard would make this a dream office, a place he could write many more bestsellers.

He couldn't fault the condition of anything inside the house. "The previous owners took care of everything—almost preserved it, really."

"I agree. It's a little like stepping back in time to the 1970s."

The glimpse of the kitchen earlier had shown a fraction of the room's problems. The full kitchen came in at close to a deal-breaker. Nothing in it, not a single thing, could be salvaged. He was sure it had given good service in the last forty years, probably to someone who cooked—if wear indicated use.

"Gut job," he commented with a bit of fear weaving its way into his voice.

"Agreed. You could extend the cabinets into the small breakfast nook—you probably don't need two dining areas— to turn this into a dream kitchen. Center the sink under the window to the woods. Put in double ovens. Maybe there." She pointed to the opposite side of the room.

She had a vision for the space that he could work with.

Talking fast, she added, "But I'm no designer. Hire a professional."

"The kitchen renovation scares me more than a bit, but I'd kick myself later if someone bought this out from under me."

"You still want to buy this house?" Her eyes glistened. "That's awesome!" She reached to give him a hug, then seemed to think better of it. "Let's go to my office and put the offer together. As we drive, consider the amount you want to offer."

His feelings about the house grew as they walked to the front door. When he turned to give the backyard a final glance, he knew he'd found his house. His and Emma's.

Outside, he surveyed the front. It didn't have curb appeal, but that could also be fixed.

He was glad he could afford to pour money into this house. He'd worked hard to get where he was with his writing. Some days, he wished he felt he could share the details of his second career. As an aspiring author, Holly would be able to relate. He thought about the old adage from the World War II era: Loose lips sink ships. She couldn't share with others what she didn't know.

Once they'd climbed back into her car, his convictions about this house grew to the verge of wanting to get out and stay. It felt like home. Driving away, he noticed that the neighborhood had lots of a similar size, and each house was different. Nothing cookie cutter, and that suited him well. The house vanished in the side mirror as they drove away.

By the time they pulled into her office's parking lot, he knew what to do. Inside the building, they went down a hallway to a conference room—now empty except for the long glass table with faux leather chairs surrounding it.

Holly went through the paperwork line by line on her computer. About five o'clock, people began leaving, coats on and briefcases in hand. When Holly arrived at the money section, Adam stated the amount he'd decided upon.

"But that's full price and more."

"I need a home as soon as possible. I can't imagine the land being better. Every room is large, except the small room downstairs, but I'll be happy to turn that into an office. There isn't anything inside that I can't live with as I work on it. Including that ugly kitchen."

"I think just painting the cupboards would go a long way to making it feel fresh."

He nodded. "Let's go big."

Holly hesitated. "Okay. You're my client. Let me submit this offer and call the listing agent to let him know it's on its way." She picked up her phone and stepped away. When she came back, she looked apprehensive. "They received another offer today. He couldn't say what the offer was, just that it was a great offer—and the owners were about to accept it. I'm told that they'll be moving next week, so they need to decide quickly. We'll have an answer this afternoon."

Adam leaned back in the padded chair. The house felt right to him. "Tell them I don't need a home inspection, and because it's a cash deal I can close in ten days. That gives them time to get out and not feel pressured."

"Adam," Holly said in a serious tone of voice, "a home inspector often turns up problems you didn't see. You could have foundation or roof issues, maybe something serious with the electrical or another aspect of the house."

"Land. That's my focus."

She shrugged. "Your concessions might make the difference. It's getting toward dinner time, but I've worked with this agent and know he'll pick up."

"His family must love that."

"He's another single guy. You know how they are." She gave him that smile that always warmed his heart.

Holly picked up her phone, pushed a button, and put it to her ear as she walked away again. Returning about ten minutes later, she wore a grin from ear-to-ear. "Clinched the deal. Not having to make another mortgage payment or another set of utility bills did it for them. You just bought yourself a house." She sat on the edge of the table next to him.

Adam rose to his feet and grabbed Holly, picked her up and swung her around in a circle before setting her on her feet and giving her a quick kiss. They broke apart almost as soon as it happened, and he stepped back. Walking toward the window, he stopped and whirled around. "I'm sorry I did that. I got carried away."

Holly touched her lips and stared at him, making him feel like he'd just won the jerk of the year award.

Coming back to stand in front of her, he said, "I'm genuinely sorry, Holly. I wouldn't want to make you uncomfortable."

She swallowed.

"I know we have a business relationship."

She nodded.

She seemed so shaken up that he set his hands on her shoulders and looked her in the eyes. "Are you okay?"

Instead of stepping away from him, as he had expected, she came closer. "I think I'm better than okay." Holly leaned forward and kissed him.

Adam slid his arms around her and pulled her close, deepening the kiss. When he felt her sigh, he knew his heart belonged to her. But this wasn't the appropriate setting for revealing that to her. He did the hardest thing he'd ever done and stepped away from her.

"Wow." Holly had a dazed expression.

"I agree." He'd never known a woman this open and honest. He loved that about her. He'd never been in love before. Step by step, he had taken the leap from interest to more. She'd brightened every day, made life better than it had ever been. Would he be able to make her see that they belonged together?

She kept staring at him, wonder on her face. Maybe she felt the same way.

As his surroundings came back into focus, Adam took a second step away from her. This was her place of business. A skyscraper-sized problem occurred to him. They'd just concluded the business that had brought them together. He had the house of his dreams, but not the woman.

He blurted out the first thing that came to mind. "Can I take you to dinner?"

Holly blinked and glanced around. "I don't think so. Not tonight." A nervous laugh followed, and she hit the power button on her computer and began gathering her things together.

Everything about Holly told him he wanted to spend more time with her. A lot more time. He'd have to find a way to bring them together again.

His heart said that Holly was a little bit in love with him. He had to find a way to help her see that.

Holly dropped him off at Jemma's, their routine these last couple of weeks. He brought Emma in from the backyard, and the two of them went upstairs to be out of Jemma's way. She was in the dining room doing whatever she did there.

Sitting on the chair in his room, he once again thought about the house he'd just bought. Not only did it have an amazing view, but its location was better than he could have hoped for. He paused to let the reality of the purchase sink in. The drive from Chugiak to his job at the university would be far shorter than coming from Palmer, and it was a dream compared to some of the houses she'd shown him. Having the airport nearby would be a super bonus.

The structure itself might not be the most stunning one they'd seen, but anything he didn't love could be fixed. He searched on his phone for a local florist and ordered flowers sent to Holly's house. A card with a simple "thank you" on it could be read as his happiness at her discovering a house for him. Or a response to her kiss.

Jemma called up the stairs. "Adam, I'm leaving for the day."

At the close of the front door, he grabbed his laptop and went downstairs. Jemma used the dining room table much like the desk in an office, with the addition of a sewing machine he had no idea how to use. After snapping a phone photo of everything so he would be able to put things back where he'd found them, he pushed some of her fabric to the side and set up his computer, settling down for a writing session.

Holly got to share her business triumphs with friends. His writing life, what he really saw as a business since he self-published, had to remain a secret. Out of all the people in his life, she was the one he most wanted to tell. He'd wait a little longer to see if their relationship grew closer.

Chapter Fourteen

Holly grabbed her phone to silence it, then saw Adam's picture. *Please, please don't let him be calling to cancel the contract.*

"Hello, Adam."

"Do you have a minute?"

She checked the time on her phone. A minute was about all she had. "I don't want to sound rude, ever, but I'm waiting for a client at a house."

"So you may need to get off the phone quickly."

"Exactly. I need to thank you for the bouquet of flowers. I've never had a client send flowers." He'd read her right because the mix of purple and pink suited her personality. They'd arrived on her doorstep the day after they'd found his house—and the day after their fabulous kiss. The floral scent had filled her home and reminded her of him whenever she stepped through the door.

"I'm glad they made you happy. Have you ever gone dipnetting for salmon?"

"That's a question from out of left field." Kind of like asking if she'd ever skied Alyeska without asking if she skied. "Yes, I make sure I go at least once every summer."

"Would you like to go with me? I'll take care of everything."

Was he asking her out on a date? After weighing the pros and cons of dating Adam O'Connell, she decided she liked the idea. He had gone from strict professor to potential suitor. Maybe more than potential. Her heart raced as she remembered yesterday's kiss.

"Think of it as my thank you for finding me a house."

So much for romance. "My schedule is too tight to take a couple of days off."

"How about one? Or most of a day?"

His wanting to spend time with her must mean they had more than a professional relationship—that his kiss didn't spring from the joy of winning the real estate bidding war. Maybe partly, but she didn't think he would have kissed *any* female real estate agent.

"Adam, the drive back and forth would take most of the day. Add in stops for lunch and breaks, and it would be the whole day. I'm too busy to take all that time off."

"By plane, Holly."

"*Right.* That idea is still new to me." A day with Adam might clarify her feelings. Checking her schedule, she saw that if she moved one viewing the following afternoon to the next day, she could spend time with Adam—and get some fish for her freezer. If her girls had been home, she would have needed a sitter, but she had four days until her happy chaos returned. "Tomorrow?"

"If you pick me up at eight, we can be standing hip deep in the water by noon, probably earlier."

"Those nets are big. How are we going to fit them in the plane?"

"We can borrow two from my parents."

Holly pulled up in front of Jemma's old house, currently Adam's, where she found him waiting outside. She drove to Merrill Field and pulled in next to his Cessna. She felt like a true Alaskan knowing the plane's make. Adam began his preflight while Holly went to the trunk to get her chest waders, a lunch she'd packed for them in a small ice chest, and a much larger ice chest for their catch.

When she walked up to him, he glanced from the engine to the boots in her arms. "I've never met a woman with her own chest waders."

She raised an eyebrow. "Maybe you haven't known the right woman. Jemma has waders too."

"Bree?"

"Wouldn't be caught in them because they're usually only used in rugged places. And Bree avoids anything that even hints of wilderness if she can."

He dropped a quick kiss on her lips, startling her—but making her happy down to her toes. "Thank you for joining me today."

"Anytime."

He stared at her, probably wondering if she referred to the kiss or their upcoming day. She'd definitely meant the kiss.

He finished his inspection, and they were soon taxiing toward the runway, then airborne. Her second flight felt more natural than the first. With one flight to her credit, she felt more like a seasoned small plane passenger. Until she looked out the window and gasped in awe. "I've been on the

Kenai at ground level for years, but this takes my breath away." She watched the rivers and lakes pass under their plane. "When you drive here, you see pieces of civilization along the road. It's really a wilderness."

"Without many people. I know. I don't tire of the view."

Too quickly, they landed in Kenai and tied down. Adam's father met them at the plane in a large pickup truck.

He gave her a long glance, but Adam only introduced her as Holly Harris, his real estate agent who deserved a treat after putting up with him. The older man remained silent as they drove, then pointed to the nets in the garage once they'd arrived, before vanishing through a door into his house.

Adam grabbed the long-handled nets and a pair of boots for himself, hustling them out to the back of the truck. Holly wanted to ask Adam why he was in such a hurry, but she would have had to grab his arm to make him slow down long enough. He kept glancing at the house as he worked.

"Why are you in a crazy hurry?"

He leaned over and said in a low voice, "Let's get out of here fast—before my father has a chance to tell my mother that I've brought a beautiful woman home with me."

Warmth rushed through her. "Beautiful?"

"Of course," he hissed. "Now, hurry." He hustled her down the driveway and over to the truck's passenger side. As she put on her seatbelt and Adam raced around the truck to get into the driver's seat, she noticed a woman striding purposefully toward them from the direction of the house. He started the truck and pulled away before the woman was halfway down the long driveway.

Holly fought against a grin but lost the battle. "You're afraid of your mother."

Silence greeted her. He finally answered. "Fear isn't the right word. It's more that I didn't want her to grill the two of us about our *relationship*."

Well, that sure shut her up. Did they have a relationship? They'd shared more than one kiss. Make that two kisses. One that had sent fireworks into the sky. Time to change the subject. "Adam, I've gone dipnetting on the Kenai River. It must be closer. Why the Kasilof?"

"Fewer people. And I prefer the smaller scale of it. The Kenai River sometimes reminds me of the busyness of tailgating after a football game. Not that the Kasilof is completely off the beaten track—but there is a significant difference."

He stopped at a store and went in to get a bag of ice that he loaded into the ice chest she'd brought. After driving for a few more miles, they turned off onto another paved road that eventually ended at a parking lot beside a wide, flat gravel bank leading to a river.

When they pulled into a space, Holly saw what he'd meant about the location. The wide shoreline was dotted with people, but they weren't crowded into the water.

"Adam, I have a feeling this will be packed this weekend. It helps that we're here on a Monday."

"It certainly does. This is a moment when I'm glad I have summers off."

Holly excitedly pulled on her chest waders. She picked up one of the nets—a mesh area four or five feet across, with a telescoping handle longer than the truck—and waddled over to the river which flowed into the salt water of Cook Inlet within her sight. Adam geared up and headed out into the water upstream from her. She braced herself as she stepped into the current and waded out until the water reached about waist level.

A boat roared by farther out in the river, its net in the water. She dropped hers into the current, holding on against the force of the water and waited for a fish to swim into it. A salmon bumped into her leg as it made its way upstream, something that always gave her a sense of awe. This was her Alaska. She wished visitors could experience dipnetting, but regulations limited it to residents.

They took occasional breaks, once to eat the sandwiches and slices of pie she'd brought. Within a few hours, they'd reached their limit—both of salmon and the exhilarating experience. Holly offered, but Adam insisted on cleaning their catch. On the road back to his parents' house, Adam fell silent.

"Is everything okay? We had an amazing day here, right?"

He gripped the steering wheel tightly. "I'm wondering if I should park my plane closer to my temporary residence at Jemma's old house, in case I want to do more salmon fishing. Why don't I fly you to Merrill Field so you can drive back in your car? Then I'll move my plane to the Palmer airport."

She shrugged. "Okay. I can do that."

That didn't resolve the tension. In fact, it appeared to grow with each mile. "What's really wrong, Adam?"

He blew out a breath. "I've realized my dad has to take us back to the airport."

"That makes sense." After a moment, she figured out what he meant. "And your mother will be waiting to meet me when we arrive."

"Like a mosquito buzzing and looking for its next victim."

She cringed.

"Maybe not the best analogy. Let's just say that I've experienced this for half my life, since I was a teenager and brought home my first girlfriend. My brothers would all agree. It doesn't get easier."

"Am I your girlfriend?"

He twisted in his seat to look at her.

Holly groaned. "I said that out loud, didn't I? I don't do that with anyone but you."

"Well, I'd like to hope that maybe someday you might want to go out on a date with me." The usually in-control man beside her stumbled through a sentence worthy of his teenage self. "But only if you want to."

She needed to put the poor man out of his misery. Fighting a smile, she said, "Yes, I would like to do that."

Adam chuckled as he pulled the truck onto what she recognized as his parents' road. "I wasn't at my most suave, was I?"

Holly shook her head slowly. "Perhaps not. But the sentiment was there." She reached over and took his hand in hers. "Would you like to go to dinner tomorrow night?"

He glanced at her with a stunned expression. "You're asking me?"

"It seemed like a good idea."

"Since I wasn't doing the asking?" At her nod, he said, "Yes, I would."

Adam pulled into his parents' driveway and turned off the truck. He didn't appear to be in a rush to get out. As Holly popped open the door, his mother stepped outside. Instead of rushing like earlier, she casually approached. She knew they were trapped here until someone returned them to the airport.

Once introductions were out of the way, his mother none-too-subtly said, "My son's quite a catch—don't you think, Holly?"

Holly smiled. "Almost as good as the salmon we got today."

His mother did a double-take. "Do you like salmon, Holly?"

"Yes, ma'am. It's one of my favorite things."

The older woman glanced from her to her son, and back again. Then she turned and headed toward the house. "Why don't you come inside to wash off your fishy hands? I have coffee made if you'd like a cup—or Howard can take you right to the airport."

Holly answered for them. "I still have to work tonight, so we'd better get going."

Once their hands were clean, Adam's mother asked his father to take them to the airport. The older man stood from his place on the couch and took out his keys. Adam tensed up, probably waiting for embarrassing comments or questions.

His mother smiled. "Have a safe flight home."

Adam's mouth worked up and down, like a fish out of water. He followed his father out the door with a glazed expression on his face.

After his father had dropped them off at his plane and driven away, Adam said, "Mom liked you. That's the only explanation."

"The feeling was mutual. I like a woman who speaks her mind."

Adam gave her a thoughtful look. She was beginning to hope he appreciated that quality in a woman too. Now, there was just one little matter to take care of. Make that two—Abbie and Ivy. They'd be home in three days. Between now and then, she had to find a way to tell Adam about her girls.

And hope he liked the idea of dating a woman with kids.

Then again, maybe she would just wait.

Chapter Fifteen

Holly turned onto the road to Jemma's house. She hadn't had a chance to tell her sister about her dipnetting day with Adam, and the fact that she seemed to be dating him. She wouldn't have considered that possible yesterday morning, but today it was true.

As she rounded the curve, Jemma's business office loomed ahead. Or rather, the RV parked in the driveway loomed ahead. Instead of bringing her kids directly to her house in two days—as promised—her parents had driven to Jemma's today. Abbie and Ivy were home.

She whipped into the drive beside the RV, hopping out of her car and hurrying around the vehicle. She followed the sound of voices she knew belonged to her kids. They played tag with Jemma in the front yard.

When Ivy spotted her, she yelled, "Mommy!" and raced her direction. Abbie turned and followed her sister. Holly knelt and wrapped her arms around her girls, holding them close.

Jemma's voice sounded from above. "Mom and Dad didn't realize someone was living here. They thought it was empty, and that they could use the whole house."

Holly jerked her head up to see her sister towering over her.

The girls pushed to be released. "We're going to play more."

"Go ahead." Holly stood, and her girls ran off across Jemma's front yard. "I didn't think about Adam when I saw the RV." Excitement over having her girls back in her life played tug-of-war with Adam discovering they existed before she told him. Holding onto this secret might have been a monumental mistake.

She hurried around the RV to where she'd parked her car. Adam's motorcycle was nowhere to be seen. *Whew.*

The pattern this summer was for her parents to stay here for an hour or two before moving on to their next stop. Adam was out, so he would probably not meet her kids today.

This time, a man wouldn't be able to dismiss her because she had kids. He would love her first, as she was starting to love him. *Then* she'd tell him about her kids, and he could learn to love them too. That was her plan, and she was sticking to it.

Love? Love! She flopped against the RV, leaning into that solid vehicle for support. She could *not* be falling for her former professor. *No.*

Laughter. He'd won her over with laughter. And who could ignore a flight on a beautiful day? What about the flowers he'd sent to thank her for her hard work? She didn't doubt that he felt something for her, but was it more than a passing interest?

Feeling weak, she sank to the ground. The gravel drive bit into her knees.

"Holly?" Jemma's concerned voice called from above. Then her sister crouched beside her. "Are you all right? Should I call Bree?"

She managed a slight shake of her head. "It's Adam," she whispered.

"Has he been injured?"

She stared into her sister's eyes. "Not that I know of. Jemma, I might be falling in love with the man."

Jemma laughed. "Oh, that. I've known about it for a week. Maybe longer."

"A week?" She heard the screech in her voice, and that brought her to her feet. "I can't love this man."

Jemma stood. "Is that fact or hope?"

"Jemma, love hurts here." Holly tapped her chest. "I can't have that pain again. I'm not even sure I loved Grant, and that hurt. Losing Adam could be worse." *Much worse.*

Her sister put her hand on her arm. "It doesn't have to hurt. Look at your sisters, your parents. One man was a jerk."

"What about Matt?"

"I liked Matt. But love wasn't involved. He was convenient."

She pushed on her chest. "It hurt when he left town."

"For how long? You mentioned Matt for a day or two after the great kiss-off. Then you moved on. You made getting over him look easy. That *isn't* love."

"I'd wanted so much from him. A life with him and the girls."

"Your girls get to meet Adam today. I suspect everything will be fine."

"No. No. No! I need to divert him, maybe give him an errand." She pulled her phone out of her purse.

"To last the rest of the week? Are you planning to send him to Seattle for a loaf of bread?"

"The week?"

"Yes. Mom and Dad need to have repairs made on the RV's engine. Something about it stuttering on hills."

Holly stomped her foot in frustration. "I love my girls. You know I do." She stared at Jemma, and her sister nodded. "I wouldn't trade a second of the time I've been their mom for anything. I just wanted a man to love me for me this time." Turning away, she added, "I don't want to wonder if he's choosing me or my kids. Or rejecting me or my kids."

"And now, instead of that pretend love with Matt, you're in love with a man who didn't know about the girls."

"*Didn't* know?" She turned to face her sister again. "That's an odd choice of words."

"Not really." She pointed to the motorcycle that rounded the curve.

Holly wheeled around, giving a half wave to Adam as he found a spot for his motorcycle next to her car.

"Stick here with me, please. I feel a little like I'm facing a firing squad."

Jemma gave her a quick hug. "Give him a chance. The house he's living in is filled with people he hasn't met, including our parents and your girls, who can charm the birds out of the sky."

Dread twisted inside her, threatening to overwhelm any joy she felt at having her family nearby again. Introducing a man to your parents usually hit monumental on the dating scale. She'd rarely brought a boy home for her parents' intense, but kind, inspection. Adding not one child but two—a matching pair of precocious never-knew-what-they'd-say five-year-olds—to the event would make this a day Adam O'Connell might remember forever.

Adam swung his leg over to dismount his motorcycle as a few, small raindrops spritzed down. Now that he had his house, he needed to move buying a car to the top of his to-do list.

The scene in front of him felt off. Holly's tentative wave, Jemma with her arm around her sister—and both of them standing next to a large RV he'd never seen before. Holly had once mentioned her parents were touring Alaska in an RV, so he may have a gauntlet to run. Children's voices, those of little girls, talked and laughed beyond the RV.

He guessed that Holly's family had come to visit. He'd met her sisters, though, and was certain neither of them had children. Jemma didn't. Bree had just had a secret marriage, and she and her new husband were currently in New York City for a few days. No one had mentioned kids. These had to be the kids from the photos in Holly's hallway—from a cousin or someone like that.

A matched set of blonde-haired little girls ran over to Jemma. "Auntie Jemma!" one said. Holly gave him a glance, then gave the girls a sweet smile. Jemma swung the girl who'd spoken into the air, then lowered her back to the ground.

"There's a puppy in the backyard!" the other girl said, bouncing on her feet with excitement.

How could Jemma be their aunt? He didn't know whose kids they were. They were cute, though. "She isn't a puppy. She's a full-grown dog."

At his words, they raced over to him.

One said, "But she's so tiny."

"That's as big as she will be. Her name's Emma."

"I'm Abbie. This is my sister Ivy." Abbie extended her hand.

"I'm Adam, and I'm pleased to meet you." He took her hand and solemnly shook it. When he did that, Ivy extended hers and he did the same. With the formalities over, he asked, "Would you like to meet Emma?"

Ivy nodded. "Yes, sir." She put her small hand in his right hand, then Abbie put her hand in his left. A little tug near his heart surprised him. He'd never thought of himself as a kid person, but he could tell these two were special. He didn't see how he would ever tell them apart in the future—if he ever saw them again after today—but with one identified on each side of him, he could manage right now.

The two girls tugged him toward the backyard. He dug in his heels to slow the pace when he reached Holly and Jemma. Holly's face had gone so pale that he did a double-take. Were these girls the family secret? Maybe they belonged to a fourth sister no one talked about.

Jemma spoke. "They're a handful."

"We're sweet as little angels. Gramma said so."

Both women laughed.

Holly remained silent, but Jemma spoke again. "Be gentle with the dog, okay?"

Abbie nodded. "We learned with Chloe. Right, Ivy?"

"Yes. And this dog is so small it's like a toy. We could even dress her up in some of our dolls' clothes."

Adam felt a surge of panic. He leaned over to their level. "Emma wouldn't like that."

"Okay." The little girl shrugged, much like Holly would have at that moment. "Could she wear a bow?"

His mother had bought a jacket for Emma, and the dog had struggled to get it off the second he'd fastened it. He didn't believe an accessory would fare better. Compromise did appear necessary, though. "She's never worn a bow, so I'm not sure that would make her happy. Maybe you could help me choose a pretty new collar for her."

The two girls looked at each other. Ivy answered, "We'd like that."

"Pink with sparkles?" Abbie asked, hope in her voice.

He stifled a shudder. "Remember that I'm a boy, and I have to take her out. Could we find something that's pretty but didn't sparkle?"

A big sigh from Ivy, again just like one from Holly, told him she didn't love the idea. "Sparkly is best, but Mommy says we have to com-pro-mise sometimes." She said the big word slowly but seemed to know what it meant.

"She's right." Adam nodded solemnly. Bless her, this mysterious mother.

The girls pulled him again.

He said, "I guess we're going to see a dog."

Jemma grinned, and Holly gave what he'd have to call a nervous laugh. What had he stepped into the middle of? Holly looked about ready to jump out of her skin.

Emma bounced and barked happily when she spotted her owner. The trio came to a stop at the gate to the chain-link fence that marked Emma's new play space. He lifted the latch, swung it open, and they entered. "Watch your step for—"

"We know. Chloe makes messes too." Ivy giggled. "But Emma's will be smaller messes, right?"

He laughed. "I'm sure of that." He picked Emma up and held her to his chest. She swiped her tongue across his cheek. "Emma, I have two new friends for you to meet." She gave a single, happy bark as though she understood. "Abbie and Ivy—is your last name Harris or something else?"

One little girl said, "Harris."

He continued, "This is Emma O'Connell."

Abbie reached toward the dog but paused halfway. "Can we pet her?"

"Emma likes meeting new people, so she'd be happy to have you pet her." He crouched so they could more easily reach the dog.

When the little girl rubbed Emma, she received a tongue across her arm in thank you. Giggling, she petted her again.

"My turn." The girls traded places. Once he saw that they would be gentle with his dog, he set her on the ground. The girls crowded around her, but he watched them for any sign of overzealousness in their affection.

"Grandpa, look at the little dog," one of them said, looking up to Adam's left.

Adam turned toward that direction and found the older man standing there watching them, their grandfather. If Jemma was their aunt, this had to be Holly's dad or stepdad.

"They're used to dogs and cats, son. You won't need to worry. Well, there was the time they dressed Bree's cat Stitches up as a butterfly last summer when they were taking care of him. How kids that age managed the logistics of wings amazes me. They said something about copying what their Aunt Jemma had made them. They didn't hurt him, but the poor cat acted embarrassed and raced around the room a couple of times after we'd set him free."

"The girls and I had a discussion about costumes, and agreed on just a new collar."

The older man nodded. "Then you're fine. They're great kids, and I haven't known them to disobey a clear directive. Now, if you've left any loopholes open, they'll find them. Those two girls are five going on seventeen. There's a bit of teenager in them." He extended his hand. "James Harris. Do you know one of my daughters?"

"Adam O'Connell. Holly is my real estate agent. My townhouse was damaged in a fire, and I lost everything. Jemma took pity on me when she learned I'd bunked with a fellow professor and that had gone awry. She's letting me stay in a guest room here." Should he ask the man who the girls belonged to? That could be a touchy, family-only, subject.

"Professor, you say? I teach biology in Tennessee."

"English, in Anchorage." Emma's happy barks told him she'd found friends. "I was fortunate to have Holly as my student in two classes."

"Uh huh." The man nodded slowly, as though evaluating him and then deciding he was a life-form worthy of further contact.

Adam broke eye contact with the man to make sure the girls and his dog were okay. One of them sat on the ground with Emma in her lap, Abbie, he thought, because she'd been wearing a slightly darker shade of pink. Or was that Ivy?

"Holly worked hard to get through school. Her mother and I are proud of her. Having her mother's aunt give her the house helped, but being a single mother and going to school wasn't easy."

The one in the lighter pink stretched out on the ground. Emma climbed onto her, licking her cheek, while both girls giggled. "Right. College can be work." His mind latched onto the full sentence, and he swung around toward the man. "Abbie and Ivy are Holly's children?"

The man's expression said Adam had dropped a notch from his earlier evaluation. "Jemma married last winter. And Bree married Michael last month. They don't have children yet."

Holly, married? Adam's heart dropped to somewhere around his knees and rolled around there, struggling to continue beating.

As he fought for air, Holly's father added, "Her mother and I wish she had a man in her life."

Taking slow breaths, Adam leaned against the wood siding on the old house. *Not married. She just has children.* He wasn't sure how that sat with him. Sure, people made mistakes. God knew he had. But he didn't have children to show for any of his.

Holly warily stepped up to the fence. Her father took one look at her, glanced Adam's way, then walked away in a hurry. Smart man.

Her expression of near panic told him that she probably hadn't planned this meeting.

He had two options. Be a jerk and leave because she hadn't mentioned kids. Their relationship had been professional until he'd bought his house, so her back story hadn't been expected then.

Or, he could be a good guy. Later, there would be time to decide if he wanted Holly with these two strings attached. "I'm not going to judge your past. You aren't the only one who ever have had a youthful indiscretion."

"Well, thank you, Dr. O'Connell." She kept her eyes on her girls, but he could clearly hear the hard edge in her voice.

Adam took a step back.

"You sanctimonious oaf. I didn't have a youthful or any other type of indiscretion, as you so delicately put it. The girls are the product of a marriage."

Marriage? Holly had been *married* before? "But you and your girls share the last name of Harris."

"He walked out on us when he learned I wasn't just pregnant, but pregnant with twins. He'd never wanted children—seemed to have decided to put up with just the one—but concluded that two crossed the line for him. When the divorce finalized before their birth, I left him and his name out of our life."

"What about child support?"

"I wouldn't take a dime from a man who didn't want those beautiful children. He hasn't tried to contact me, and I haven't bothered him. We'd talked about traveling, and last I heard, he was teaching English in Japan. I didn't plan those girls, but I love them with every fiber of my being." Her breath hitched as if she were near tears. Then she gathered herself together, seeming to grow taller, and gave him a glare that told him she'd cause him pain if he ever said anything disparaging about her children.

"You have two great girls. You've done an excellent job."

At those words, her anger diffused a notch, and she became more like the woman he knew. And loved.

Glancing toward the RV, he noticed that her father watched them, and had a readiness about him that Adam knew to fear. This woman had been through a lot, and her father wasn't going to allow another man to hurt her.

Blocking out the older man, he put his hand on Holly's shoulder. She looked up, into his eyes. "Holly, I'm sorry—but I need to take time to figure out how I feel."

"I want to ask, 'What do you mean?' But I get it. You don't know if you want to continue to develop a relationship with me." Her eyes turned sad. "This won't be the first time I've had that happen."

He glanced toward her father and saw that he was watching even more carefully now. "I have a place I go to think things through. I just need to breathe."

She nodded and tried to smile, but the sadness didn't pass.

"I'm not leaving the state or anything. I found the Swan Lake Canoe Route not long after my parents moved to Kenai."

"Swan Lake? I took the girls there last year. I can see why you'd feel that way."

"Swan Lake? We loved it there, didn't we, Abbie?"

He turned to peer over his shoulder in the direction the voice had come from and found the two girls standing a few feet away from him and their mother.

Abbie agreed. "Yes. Mommy let us help carry things when we had to cross from one lake to the next one."

Ivy added, "But not the canoe. Mommy always asked a grown-up to help her carry the canoe."

"Swan Lake?" a male voice asked.

Adam's head swiveled to the left, giving him the feeling that he was at a tennis match. Holly's father had returned, now wearing a more jovial expression.

"Jemma, Holly, and I went through it when they were kids. Bree was at a summer camp. I'm glad you're going. When do you leave?" His gaze went from him to Holly, and then the girls.

Holly held up her hands to protest, but before she'd said a word, another voice chimed in.

"You'll have so much fun!" In the chaos, Holly's mother had joined her husband outside the fence.

Adam nodded. "Yes, ma'am. It's always fun."

The girls danced with glee. One of them—he decided he couldn't tell them apart—said, "Mommy told us we couldn't go there again this summer. We're so glad she changed her mind!"

Mrs. Harris put her finger on her lips as she considered the situation. "You'll either need two canoes or one long canoe."

Adam found himself answering. "My parents have both options. They love canoeing."

"Where do they live?" her father asked.

"Kenai."

"Well, that's perfect isn't it, Maggie?"

Stepping through the gate, Holly's mother herded Holly and the girls back out of it. "Let's get you packed up in a hurry. Your father and I wanted to relax for a few days. We'll take over Jemma's house. Not that we wouldn't happily share with you, Adam." Holly glanced over at him and shrugged helplessly, then followed her mother and daughters.

Mrs. Harris said, "Your car is a bit small for all of the gear the four of you will need."

"Mom, Adam has a plane at the Palmer airport."

"All the pieces have fallen into place, haven't they?" With that, the group turned a corner past the RV and out of his sight.

"A force of nature," Mr. Harris said.

Adam shook his head to clear it. "Excuse me, sir?"

"My wife, Maggie. She's a force of nature. Don't worry, son. She'll have the three of them packed up quickly, and you'll be able to get on your way."

"But sir—"

"I know. You'd probably rather take Holly alone on the trip. We prefer for her to have two little chaperones."

"It isn't that, but—"

"You'll have a wonderful time. I'd better get our things unloaded and into Jemma's house before my wife returns. She'll want to take a shower and change after a week in an RV. One learns these things after years of marriage." He gave Adam a conspiratorial wink, one that Adam interpreted to mean he would soon learn what the older man meant.

Chapter Sixteen

The plane took off a few minutes after noon. Holly held onto the edges of her seat as land and wheels disconnected. She'd tried to redirect her mother, but every word she'd said and everything she'd done had pushed them further down this apparently unchangeable path.

"This is fun, Mommy," Ivy said from the back seat.

"We have to fly a lot more." Abbie agreed in her childlike way, not understanding that it was unlikely the three of them would be in a small plane again, once Adam had safely returned them to Palmer in three days.

She had assumed she'd experienced her one and only flight, then there'd been a second one to go dipnetting. Hope had made her think she and Adam had a future, but he'd barely spoken to her since meeting Abbie and Ivy. Credit where credit was due: he'd been kind to her girls, and hadn't let his anger toward her shift onto them.

Mountains passed quickly by on her left, reminding her of how lovely it was to fly to their destination. Eliminating hours of road travel with two small girls would be enough incentive to buy a plane if her budget allowed. Which it didn't.

The girls happily pointed out things they flew over. She was grateful for the calm air that didn't give them a reason to be afraid during their first flight in a small plane.

Twenty minutes later, Adam turned to the girls for a moment, pointing over his shoulder. "There's the Kenai airport." Turning back around, he added, "We're almost there." He spoke into his headset a minute later, and they soon landed and taxied to a stop. The craziness of the day continued when Adam's father stepped out of his truck as Adam tied down his plane.

"Dad, these are Holly's girls, Abbie and Ivy."

Adam's father rubbed his chin. "You're taking the whole family out with you?"

Adam gave a single nod. She'd like to give him an out, but she didn't have the cash for a hotel. They were at his mercy at this point.

Abbie met the older man halfway. "We're going to the Swan Lake Canoe Route again. Isn't that wonderfully awesome?"

Where had she picked up that expression?

The man bent over to her height, just as Adam had when he'd spoken with her girls. "It sure is. I have a canoe that all of you can fit in." Standing, he said, "Adam, you can borrow my truck again. You'll all fit in there."

Now, *his* father was in on it. Her parents didn't know his—otherwise, she'd smell a conspiracy.

Holly dipped her paddle into the water to the right of the canoe. Pausing for a second, she rested the paddle across her lap and pinched her leg. Giving a low yelp, she shook her head. This was real. She sat in a canoe with Abbie and Ivy . . . and Adam on the first of the more than two dozen lakes that comprised the Swan Lake Canoe Route. Each connected to the next with a waterway, or what canoers called a portage—a hike, sometimes short, sometimes long, experienced while carrying a canoe and gear. Now in part of the massive Kenai National Wildlife Refuge, they'd seen the last of civilization for a while.

The girls, wearing life vests like her and Adam, sat in the center of the boat on the floor of the canoe. He had stowed the large, waterproof bags of gear in front of and behind them. Two tents, four sleeping bags, a camp stove, food—everything they'd need for two nights on the trail. Without a word about the fact that she now had two children, Adam's father had outfitted them from the veritable sporting goods store in his garage.

Adam pointed to their left, so she switched and paddled on the left side, sending the canoe that direction as the lake's contour changed and the boat needed to turn. Holly shook herself. If ever she needed to be alert, it was now, on the water with her girls.

She'd eaten breakfast. Normal. Gone to Jemma's. Normal. Her parents had arrived. Still fairly normal. Spending time with her girls satisfied something deep inside her. If only she'd thought ahead at that moment, been quicker to find a way to send Adam away for the day, this excursion wouldn't have happened. She'd be home, maybe enjoying a cup of cocoa and a good book, and watching her girls play. Or at the park with them. Tonight, she and Adam would have gone to dinner. She might have found the courage to tell him about Abbie and Ivy.

So, then, what had happened?

Adam had ridden up on his motorcycle. Her parents must have decided he seemed a likely candidate for a husband. They'd never push them together like this if they hadn't. She had to admit to feeling more than a little shocked that they'd sent them off into the wilderness together.

"Mommy, there's a big moose and a little moose over there." Abbie pointed to their left, fortunately far enough away that her girls wouldn't be in any danger when they got out.

Moose were cute, and she'd heard many stories from people who had grown up in Alaska who'd been almost nose to nose with one with no trouble. But she also knew that as with most mamas, they would get after anything that threatened their babies.

As the canoe skidded onto land, Adam put on rubber boots and stepped out. He grabbed the side near the girls and swung it slowly toward shore. He had the girls stay put. Holly pulled on similar boots and climbed out. The boots were necessary on this first portage—a small stream with barely enough water for a canoe loaded with gear and girls. They'd have to walk and pull the canoe along with a rope.

At the other side of the short stream, the adults joined the kids again and paddled across the small second lake. As they floated, Holly took a moment—the first since she'd arrived—to appreciate her surroundings. The area was almost flat, with low hills rising in places, all covered in the trees most often seen in the area—a large percentage of spruce and paper birch with some brush mixed in. Reaching the other side, they all disembarked.

"Can we help?" Ivy asked as the pile of gear on the shore grew.

Adam smiled at Ivy. "You can not only help—you're important. I need for each of you to carry something."

Both Ivy and Abbie beamed.

Adam gave each girl a small item to carry—Abbie a tarp, and Ivy a frying pan—then the adults picked up significantly heavier loads. Holly had a tent in each hand, Adam their ice chest and a bag with their food. Never leaving their food alone was best.

As they began the short march over a trail clogged with tree roots, Holly said, "Remember to watch where you're going, girls."

"Yes, Mommy," Ivy answered, stepping over roots that must have seemed giant-sized to her tiny frame.

Holly had once made this trip wearing a fully-loaded backpack with a group of friends, and that had made portaging easier. She'd have brought her backpack—if she'd had time to plan.

The dirt trail took them a short distance through trees. The weight in each hand became noticeable at about the crest of the hill. By the time the next lake came into view, her arms ached. Paddling and carrying weren't in her daily routine as a real estate agent.

Forcing a smile, Holly set the tents down at the edge of the next lake, and her arm muscles shouted, "thank you!" As soon as she stopped moving, mosquitoes swarmed. She got out the bottle of repellent and gave herself and her kids another coat of the stuff. Done with that, she prepared mentally for what remained. She wasn't a wimp, and she had decent arm muscles, but these portages weren't ever fun. Well, the pretty scenery as they walked from place to place was fun, but not the carry. And especially not the canoe carry.

"Why don't you stay here with the girls? I think I can carry the next load by myself." He leaned closer and lowered his voice, whispering against her hair and sending a thrill through her. "We probably shouldn't wear them out walking back and forth, if we can avoid it." That snapped her back to reality. The man thought like a parent.

"Have you spent time with children?" she asked.

"No. Did I do something wrong?"

"*All* right."

"A compliment?"

"A compliment." Turning to her girls, she said, "Let's check the map to see where we're going next while Adam brings us our sleeping bags."

They hurried over, one to each side of Holly, and she unfolded the paper she'd tucked into the side of a duffel bag. They'd gone this far last year, found a large enough space to pitch their tent, and spent the night. She'd thought it quite an accomplishment with two four-year-olds.

Adam left them, returning about twenty minutes later with the rest of the gear. When she started to stand, he motioned her down. "There's a party of four guys behind us. I asked if they'd help carry our canoe over, and they agreed."

"Thank you! I'll relax here—just the three of us. Or should I say three million." At his puzzled expression, she added, "Us and the mosquitoes."

Adam laughed. "They have been thick. Not that I've seen it any other way this time of year."

"I know. I love the Alaskan outdoors. Mosquitoes are just part of the landscape."

Tapping the map in her hand, she asked, "How far are you planning to go tonight?"

He frowned as he watched the girls playing near the shore—inches-deep shallow water she knew held no danger. "If we manage to be the first ones there, I've camped at an excellent site on the other side of this lake. I'm pretty sure *our* two tents would fit."

She got his meaning. "But not someone else's tent too."

Two men, probably in their early twenties, came over the top of the hill with a load of gear.

"Ready for help, old man?" One of them clapped Adam on the shoulder.

Adam hobbled along in front of them for a few steps. Laughing, the group moved out of sight. Male bonding. Holly shook her head. Stepping over to her daughters, she waited for their canoe and, she hoped, the last leg of the day's journey. She'd need to get them fed in the next hour, or fussiness would ensue. Adam might not want to be near any of them again if he experienced a hungry, cranky set of twins.

As they set up the tents on the flat area he'd mentioned next to the lake, he kept an eye on the sky. The forecast was for possible rain. He knew that could mean a few drops or a downpour. Holly caught him as he made his third weather check.

"Rain on its way?"

He sighed. "I think so. How do you keep them happy when they can't go outside?" He gestured toward the girls.

Holly grinned. "Any way you can."

He groaned.

"Don't worry."

She rested her hand on his arm, something he had to admit did pull away some of his concern.

"I have coloring books and crayons. We've had to do this before. They went on their first camping trip when they were almost two."

He breathed a sigh of relief. "Then we're okay."

"Sure. As long as it doesn't pour and turn dirt into mud."

"Last time I did the canoe trail, I wore a rain jacket and pants the whole time."

"This part of Alaska does do a nice drizzle, doesn't it?"

He laughed. "That it does." He pointed to the hill rising beyond their tents. "We'll be sleeping in puddles if it does pour."

"Abbie and Ivy would love to make a trench on the side of the tent facing the hill. It'll keep them happy, and will direct the water away if it's a little more than a drizzle."

"I've been considering doing that, but planned to take care of it myself."

She brushed away his comment with a wave. "Let them do it. Let's just hope all we get is a drizzle, and we don't need it."

Adam fought to find a comfortable position in his sleeping bag. Finally lying flat, he counted the seams on the tan fabric of his tent's roof and tried to sort out his day. And his life. The beauty of camping mid-summer in Alaska was that you didn't need a flashlight. The downside was that nothing told his exhausted body it needed to sleep. He willed his muscles to relax, going through them one-by-one as best as he remembered from high school biology.

There didn't appear to be one person to blame for his current predicament. The tent next door held a woman he was more than a little in love with. A woman with children! Sure, they were cute kids. He liked Abbie and Ivy. But he didn't have a choice, and he didn't like being told he had to do anything. If he wanted the woman in his life, he had to take the kids too. Could he do that? Each time he tried to picture him and Holly together, the scene froze, and the two kids jumped into it.

Not to mention, if he did decide he wanted a deeper relationship with her—despite the kids—he'd have to tell her about his writing. It had become part of who he was.

Tiny drops of rain landed on the tan fabric overhead. Light rain would make the morning air fresh and clean. The slow melody of the raindrops began untangling the confusion in his mind, doing what his relaxation technique hadn't. His eyelids growing heavy, he closed them.

The sound of a train barreling down on him brought Adam to his knees. Blinking, he reached for the zipper on the tent's door and stopped. There wasn't a train track anywhere on the Kenai Peninsula, other than the tracks from Anchorage to Seward, probably a hundred miles away.

Wind buffeted the tent, pulling against the stakes. The delicate, gentle, soothing raindrops had turned into something that neared a tropical storm. At least, it felt like it in here.

There were two options as he saw things. Stay in his tent and possibly have water rush under it. But even in the very unlikely scenario of the water tugging his tent and pulling up the stakes, he had nowhere to wash to beyond the shallow shore of a small lake. Or he could step outside and try to pack up in—checking his watch he saw two a.m. on the dial—the middle of the night.

Settling back into his sleeping bag, he chose the possibility of staying dry. And he hoped the adrenaline rush of an imaginary oncoming train didn't keep him awake.

Holly's voice, from the direction of her tent, cut through the storm. "Adam."

"Yes?"

"Are we okay?"

"I think so. Are you and the girls?"

He could hear her smile in her voice. "We're fine. Yell at me if you think we need to do something."

He sincerely hoped that wouldn't be necessary. He'd pack them up and get out of here in the morning. Doing that task in mud sounded less and less appealing.

Adam felt a chill and reached for his blanket, coming back instead with a handful of something slippery. He opened his eyes and saw a sleeping bag. Right. Camping with Holly *and her girls.* As he turned onto his side, the pad under his sleeping bag rolled like the water bed he'd once slept on at his unconventional uncle's house. He rubbed his eyes and struggled to clear his head. Water sloshed underneath him as he sat up.

After unzipping the flap on his tent, he peered out and up to low, gray clouds. When he extended his hand through the opening in the mosquito netting, no raindrops landed on it.

Their window of opportunity was now, before the sky opened up again. He needed to get all of them back to the truck. The day was cool enough—probably in the low sixties—that being wet would also bring the danger of hypothermia. He now had two five-year-old girls in his care.

Adam tugged on clothes, then sat and quickly pulled on his hiking boots. After rolling up his sleeping bag and pad, he stuffed the other loose gear into his duffel bag and climbed out of the tent to find Holly already out, gathering their gear.

"Are the girls up?" Giggling from nearby gave Adam his answer.

"They are. We're getting out of here, right?" She shoved the frying pan into its bag. "I think the sky will be falling again soon."

"Yes, I want to be out of here as soon as possible."

"Oooh," one of the girls—Abbie?—said as she stepped out her tent. "We're leaving?" She jutted out her lip in a pout. Adam knew to stay out of the conversation. No man wanted to take on a female in a bad mood.

"Ivy, it's not safe to stay here. We'll come back again as soon as we can." So he still couldn't tell them apart.

"Promise?" the other girl, obviously Abbie this time, asked as she joined her sister. Both girls wore their hair pulled back in a hot-pink elastic thing like Emma had found at Holly's house.

"I promise. And I always keep my promises, don't I?"

Ivy's lip returned to normal. "Can we help?"

With the pout gone, Adam said, "We *need* your help, Ivy. You too, Abbie."

"Adam's right." Holly gave him a sweet smile, and he felt like he'd scaled Mount McKinley. "I need for both of you to gather everything inside the tent and put it back in the bag. Then I'm going to have you help me roll up our sleeping bags."

"Okay, Mommy," Abbie said, and the two of them ducked back inside.

They soon had the canoe loaded. As he helped the first girl into the canoe, she complained, "Mr. Adam, I'm hungry." His gaze flew to Holly, who reached into her pocket, pulled out a snack bar, and tore the package open before handing it to her daughter. Before the second twin asked—he wasn't even going to try guessing who was who— she repeated the process, giving it to that girl as he settled her into the canoe.

"Me too." He grinned at Holly, who surprised him when she reached into her pocket a third time.

"I set aside four because I knew we couldn't stop to eat." Leaning closer, she said, "Thank you for taking such good care of us."

Adam pocketed the snack bar, not surprised to see that it contained chocolate. What was it with women and chocolate? He'd stop to eat it on the other side of the lake. Then he realized he'd have to push through with no breaks until he got to the truck, so he pulled it out and took a bite that included chocolate chips. "Yum—right, girls?"

They both nodded. "Mommy loves chocolate," one said.

"And so do we," the other one added.

They both nodded again, quite seriously this time.

He gave a quick walk through their campsite, checking for anything they might have set to the side, finding nothing. "Let's go."

They pushed off and paddled toward the lake's opposite shore. The reverse trip took less time, their sense of urgency pushing them forward.

This time, Holly toted the canoe with him over the longer portage. He'd seen her scale the porch roof, using upper body strength that surprised him. When she picked up one of her girls and gave her a kiss, he saw where the physical strength came from. She'd been carrying the twins for a long time.

At the second to last lake, Holly called from the back of the canoe. "I think we're going to make it back without getting wet."

Adam nodded. "I've been out many times with gray clouds like these overhead and never felt a drop. But after last night, it's going to take a week for my tent to dry."

"You can pitch it in Jemma's yard. A garage would be better. Maybe I can talk Nathaniel into letting you put it in theirs."

Adam only nodded in reply. A moose and her calf, probably the pair they'd seen yesterday, stood straight ahead in the water. The animals ate grasses out of the shallows. Normally, he enjoyed watching them. Right now, his only goal was to get the two girls and their mother back to dry ground.

"Adam," Holly said with caution in her voice.

"I see them." A single drop of rain hit his face, running down his nose. Swiping his sleeve across the wet spot, he searched for options. He didn't see any other than going back to this lake's shore and pitching their tents again—not something he wanted to pursue with wet tents and more water coming down from the sky.

"Mommy, it's raining again." He heard fear in the girl's voice.

"That's okay, Ivy. We're on a wet lake, and it's just more water." At her words, a light rain began hitting them.

The mama moose, seemingly unconcerned about the weather, gave them a sideways glance, then ambled away with her offspring behind her. About twenty yards away, she dipped her head into the lake again and came up with a bite of lunch. The distance between them and the wild animals was closer than he would have liked, but waiting wasn't possible. Splitting his focus between the moose and his destination, he pushed forward, dipping the paddle in deeper and faster than before. Holly followed his lead, so they landed the canoe quickly.

As they did, he twisted to the rear and solemnly looked into the eyes of each girl. "Let's stay very quiet so we don't disturb the moose and her baby. Okay?"

"Yes, sir," they whispered in unison.

Holly added, "And don't wiggle around in your seat. We want to move very slowly so she doesn't think there's danger, and knows her baby is safe near us."

They both nodded and turned to check out the moose.

Adam and Holly stepped out and dragged the canoe to the other side of the small stream, safely avoiding the mother moose. Relief surged through him when they began paddling on the last lake. The rain began in earnest about halfway across.

Once they'd landed the canoe and everyone stood on land, he and Holly unloaded the gear and threw it in the back of the truck. He climbed into the truck bed so he could root around in one of the waterproof bags to find a large towel he knew he'd packed for just such occasions. He handed the towel to Holly, who wiped off her girls and loaded them into the truck.

Then she helped him swing the canoe upside down and slide it onto the truck's carrier. Once strapped on, he gave the tie downs a final check for security. Holly stopped him, putting her hand on his arm. "Adam, thank you for being so good with my girls. I know you didn't want to do this."

She was right. He hadn't wanted to make this trip. But, as he considered the last couple days, he realized he wouldn't have changed a thing—except the rain. "I think I can say that camping with kids is okay. They added a new dimension to it."

She laughed. "Chaos?"

He chuckled with her. "At the risk of sounding saccharine sweet, I saw things here through new eyes with them. I've been here many times, but . . ."

"They do that with everything." At that, she turned and walked toward the open passenger door, climbing inside and closing it.

Soon after they'd turned off the gravel road back onto the paved highway, Holly's phone rang. Reaching deep into the small backpack she'd traded for her usual purse, her hand felt the shape of it. Pulling the phone out on the third ring, she expected to see one of her parent's or sister's images on the screen. Matt's face stared at her. Glancing at Adam to her left, she answered it before the call went to voicemail.

"Holly, I've tried to call you since yesterday."

"We were camping."

"Oh. You're still in real estate, right?"

She had to bite her tongue to avoid a snarky comment about not much changing in the last two weeks. "Yes. Do you have a friend who wants to buy or sell a home?" Her tone held little of its former warmth.

Oblivious as usual, he continued. "I've realized that I don't need a house. I mean, it's just me, right?"

So true. "You want to sell." Should she send him to another agent? No, her heart wasn't involved. "I can help with that."

"And I want to buy a small condo. A one-bedroom."

She hesitated again. Shopping for a home involved being near Matt far more than simply listing one for sale. But why not? He'd been quite clear that they were just friends. Business was business. "Let me call you back when I get to a place where I can take notes. I'll need you to tell me what you do and don't want in your next place." They said their goodbyes and ended the call.

Holly tucked the phone in her purse and glanced over at Adam. They'd kissed. She had rather awkwardly become his girlfriend a couple of days ago. Adam hadn't asked her to dinner or anywhere else unrelated to real estate. She'd done that. Maybe the kiss hadn't mattered to him as much as it did to her. Men didn't see intimacy the same way women did. *We sink our hearts into everything we do.* Holly shook her head. "*No,*" she whispered.

"Are you okay?"

She nodded vigorously up and down. "Yeah. Uh huh. I'm fine. Thank you for asking." She'd gone and fallen for her former professor. No maybe about it anymore. Holly Harris was in love with Adam O'Connell. When had that happened, and what should she do about it? A single, slightly hysterical, laugh escaped.

Adam shot her a concerned glance.

She needed to pull herself together. She thought she'd been in love with Matt. Was she the kind of woman to rebound so quickly with another man? Being without Matt had hurt for a solid day, maybe two. Jemma was right. She'd never really loved him.

What she felt at this moment went deeper than anything she'd experienced. She had thought she'd loved her husband when she'd married him, but at this second, she wondered if it was a young love that wouldn't have endured the passage of time. It hadn't taken much to shake him from the agreed upon lifetime commitment. Children weren't exactly a surprising result of the marital relationship, after all.

The truck slowed and turned up over a slight rise and into a driveway. They'd somehow made it back to his parents' house without her noticing anything on the way. This was one of those times she was grateful for not being at the wheel.

"We're back." Ivy bounced in her seat. "And there's Grandma and Grandpa O'Connell!"

Adam gasped. "What did you call them?"

Abbie shrugged. "That's what they said to call them. Is that wrong?" She didn't like to be wrong.

"I'm just surprised." His glued-on smile told Holly "shocked" would be closer to the truth.

Holly stepped out of the truck and opened the door to the back, reaching in to unfasten her girls from their car seats. "Adam, why do you have car seats? I don't know why that didn't occur to me earlier." Maybe she did. Being railroaded into the trip had blurred much of her surroundings as she tried to process everything.

"Two of my cousins visit every summer with their kids. They have a total of four kids under the age of eight." Abbie slid to her feet, and Adam lifted her out, Ivy right behind her. Both girls hurried toward the front door and disappeared inside. Holly shut the truck's door. "So they bought the seats for when their great-nieces and nephews visit. My parents always need to be prepared. There's an assortment of seats from infant up. You said none of your brothers were married, didn't you?"

"That's right. But my mom hasn't stopped working on seeing us in wedded bliss."

She grinned. "Mine either. I'm the last one in a single state, and my parents do what they can to remedy that situation." Her gaze caught his for a few seconds, then she glanced away.

He knew as well as she did that this little trip of theirs into the wilderness had been courtesy of her parents.

"Let's find your kids and head home."

"Okay. When the storm kept me awake, I worked on my book's plot. I have a few things to add as soon as I have a quiet moment." Childish laughter sounded from inside. "Which may or may not be before the girls are in bed tonight."

When they stepped inside the house, they found Abbie and Ivy seated on stools at a kitchen counter with a sandwich, chips, and fruit on a plate in front of each. The pink and floral décor Adam had spoken about almost overpowered her as she stepped in the door.

"Mommy, Grandma O'Connell asked if we were hungry. We said we'd only had a snack bar for breakfast, and she was appalled." She said the last word carefully, then bit into her sandwich. "Ham and cheese."

Adam's mother's face colored. "I didn't mean any disrespect."

Adam spoke before she could. "There was a gap in the weather, and we had to hustle out of there before the sky opened again. Snack bars were the only option."

She nodded. "The girls are so well-mannered that I know you're a great mother. Adam's father didn't think to ask earlier, but are you two . . . ?" She pointed from her to Adam.

He'd answered the last question so well that Holly would let him handle this one.

Her girls watched with interest. "We like Adam," Ivy said. Abbie nodded.

Adam answered. "We're . . . friends?"

Holly rolled her eyes. She had plenty of men who wanted to be her friend.

His mother surprised her by not asking more. "Oh. Well, friends are always nice to have."

When the older woman busied herself in a conversation with the girls, Adam leaned over to Holly. "Maybe more than friends?"

Holly nodded and felt a silly grin cross her face. She tried to keep a straight face, but the grin persisted. She loved Adam O'Connell and maybe, just maybe, there was a chance he could love her too.

The flight back was different, but Adam assured her it was safe. It was her first of what Adam called an "instrument flight" through clouds much of the way. He had to rely on technology alone, instead of that combined with what he saw out the windows. Only a mist had squeezed out of those thick clouds, and they'd emerged into bright-blue sky on the final leg of the trip home.

She silently considered her family's future, coming to a simple conclusion about the same time they flew into sunshine. A man who didn't love her girls couldn't be part of her life. Before he'd learned about them, he'd seemed to be pursuing her. Then the air had grown chilly. His comment at his parents' house gave her hope. She prayed he wouldn't break her heart, that he did still want her—and her girls.

Once they'd landed and taxied back to the temporary tie-down Adam had used before, he shut down the engine and sat motionless as the propeller ceased its spinning. She had the feeling he had something on his mind, but after a couple of minutes, he unfastened his seatbelt and stepped out. She followed suit. He opened the door on his side, unbuckled Abbie and lifted her out, then came around to her side.

"That's a big step," Ivy commented from her seat.

Adam unbuckled her second daughter. "It is. And when you're down, you both need to be careful. Airplanes come and go here all the time, so we have to keep our eyes open."

The man had a gift with children.

They had little to unpack from the plane since most of their gear had been borrowed, so they were soon on the road back to Jemma's. As they drew ever closer to her sister and her parents, Holly decided that if her parents wanted to travel more, she'd have to ask that the girls stay with her. They'd had a wonderful trip with their grandparents, but she needed to have them near her right now.

And she had a deep desire to bake a pie and work through the idea of Adam in her life. The flavor of the pie-to-be was a mystery. The aroma of bug spray and her unwashed body after two days of hard work and mud made it clear that a stop to the store was out. Her cupboards didn't have much interesting in them, but she knew Nathaniel kept a well-stocked kitchen that she could borrow from.

A pie would give her the answers she needed. Then she'd work on her book once the girls were asleep.

Chapter Seventeen

Holly's phone rang on her drive to meet Matt in Anchorage the next morning. Adam's picture popped onto the screen, a picture she'd snapped the day before as they'd waited for his clearance to take off from the Kenai Airport. She'd had a photo of him before—she took one of every client—but that one had felt impersonal and tied to real estate shopping.

He didn't waste time with pleasantries. "Holly, can you help me shop for a couch and other furniture?"

She did want to spend time with him, but furniture wasn't her specialty.

"You don't want my new house to be a gray and brown man-cave, do you?"

Shopping for anything was far from her specialty. "Jemma's much better with decorating."

"I'm not the type to leave everything in the hands of a decorator. I want to choose the bigger pieces of furniture. I may have her help with paint and other decorating pieces."

Accessories, she thought. The man had a PhD in English but didn't know the words for decorating a house. Shopping for furniture felt intimate, personal. She rather liked the idea.

Spending time together might help her decide if love was the right emotion, or if she'd made a mistake. Baking her pie had given her time to go through everything that had happened in the last few weeks. By the time she'd put the decorative pattern of whipped cream on her strawberry pie, she'd been certain she was uncertain.

"Yes, I can help. Would you like to meet me in Anchorage in a few hours? There's a wider selection. I'm on my way to meet a client there now."

"I can do that. I thought I'd sit on Jemma's front porch and work on my computer, but today may not be the best day for that." The unmistakable sound of a saw at work sliced through the normal quiet of a morning. "I think I'll come to town and work in my office. Meet at one for lunch and then shop?"

Holly suggested the restaurant where she'd be meeting Matt and decided she'd only have coffee with her former beau, not a full meal. A couple of larger furniture stores weren't far away. Her session with Matt would be long over before Adam's arrival. Her past and her present being in the same place at the same time today might not be a good thing, so she hoped that was true.

"We should probably leave your motorcycle at the restaurant and take my car, in case you find some small pieces you'd like to take today."

"As I picture you seated behind me on my motorcycle, holding a lamp we found, I realize you're right."

Laughing, she said, "I agree. I couldn't handle that and a blender. Definitely too awkward." They ended the call with their plans set.

As trees turned into buildings and the heart of the city grew closer, Holly's phone rang. She answered without glancing at the screen. "Holly Harris."

"Holly, I've been delayed by a couple of hours. I'm needed at headquarters."

Knowing Matt was the wrong man for her had nothing to do with his profession, but being in his life had given her a whole new respect for those married to police officers. "Two hours?"

"I'll do my best." Which probably meant three hours. Maybe more.

"Text me when you're on your way." He agreed and hung up.

Holly considered her options. Adam would probably be on his way now. She pulled into a parking lot and found his number in her phone. "Adam, my client has a delay in his schedule and won't meet me for hours. Would you like to shop this morning?"

"Absolutely. I can work this afternoon. Then we can have lunch where you suggested." She gave him the name of the store, and less than an hour later, Holly pulled into the store's parking lot. She'd had enough time to stop at a bookstore and browse through the mysteries. She felt more confident about her writing when she saw that it was in line with what was on the shelves, but her work had what she thought of as the "Holly spin" on it.

She found Adam in the mattress section. A salesman stood nearby.

"I chose that one." He pointed at the mattress in front of them. "I thought I could get started with this purchase." He gave her a lopsided grin.

He thought right. She didn't want to even consider the bed. She spun on her heels. "How about couches?"

She thought she heard a chuckle, but he wasn't laughing when she looked up. A man not far from them was chuckling. "My wife wouldn't choose a bed with me when we were dating either." He grinned now.

Holly felt the heat rise all the way up her face and into her scalp. "I'm his real estate agent. I'm helping my client shop."

"Oh." He nodded, but she could tell he didn't believe her. She couldn't fault him because her words didn't ring true to her ears either.

She and Adam continued across the room. When they were surrounded by couches in pretty much every color and size imaginable, she turned to Adam. "Do you have a color scheme in mind?"

"I want earthy, dark colors."

Holly knew enough about design to view his choices all from a masculine color palette. "Your living room walls are covered in wood paneling. Are you sure you want to go that way with your colors? It might look like a cave during the darkest part of the winter." It certainly wouldn't be a color palette she'd want to live with.

Adam nodded slowly. "Let's back up. Why don't you tell me what you think would suit the room?"

She scanned the options. A contemporary model in a deep purple caught her eye. It would be the last thing he'd want in his house. "If I were to decorate a room in my book that had your wood paneling, I'd go with this." Holly pointed to one in tan leather. "Mind you, I'm not Jemma, so you're getting an untrained opinion."

Adam approached the couch, walked around it, then sat down. "Nice. It's a newer version of a man's favorite, leather. I figured you'd choose a girly fabric like that." He startled her by pointing to the purple sofa.

Holly gave a slow grin. "That one was *my* favorite, but I don't see you as a purple man."

"I'm actually okay with it. Not every guest will be a man. My mom will come, and I'd like to have some things she'd be comfortable around."

Holly didn't want to touch that. Saying something about his mother's taste in furniture wouldn't be her best bet. She couldn't help him choose an assortment of furniture that had enough flowers on it to plant a country garden. She just smiled.

"Mom's taste isn't mine."

Whew.

He asked, "What if the leather sofa was in the wood-paneled family room, and the purple one was in the upstairs living room?"

Was he trying to woo her with pretty furniture, things she would enjoy? Because it was working. But she couldn't let him turn his home into something he wouldn't want. She wasn't even sure it could all go together in the same house.

"Are you sure?" she asked. The salesman, sensing an imminent large purchase, returned and hovered at a distance.

Adam nodded.

"Could we choose furniture, take photos, and have Jemma make sure the choices are sound before you buy?"

"Of course." The hovering salesman turned away. "But I will buy the bed today. I know it's fine." The man turned back to face them, and again waited.

At that moment, the trip became fun. Each of them pointed out the pieces they liked, sat down, and tested them.

"That's hard as a rock." Adam came to his feet from the upholstered chair he'd sat on and rolled his shoulders. "I wouldn't want to spend five minutes on it."

Holly giggled. "I know. I sank into this one." She pointed to her left. "I feel like I'm inside *Goldilocks and the Three Bears*. 'This one's too hard, this one's too soft . . .'"

"As an English professor, I can embrace a literary allusion."

She wrinkled her nose. "You certainly sounded professorish right then."

"At least you understood what I meant, I hope. With that aside, have we found enough that are just right? Shopping is a necessary job, but not my favorite. I'm running out of energy."

Holly ticked off the pieces on her fingers. "Sofas, chairs, end tables, and a coffee table—to put your feet on in the family room." Glancing around, she saw the dining tables. "We haven't chosen anything for your dining room." Turning, she saw the bedroom furniture. "And you'll have a bedroom with just a bed in it." She checked her phone for the time. Matt would probably be finishing up soon. She and Adam would need to eat lunch soon.

"Considering that until today I needed everything, I'm going to count that as a success."

Adam approached the salesman and ordered the bed, scheduling the delivery for the day he'd close on the house.

Now, they just needed to get to the restaurant, order, and eat before Matt showed.

They were soon on their way to the restaurant with time to spare. Adam had said he missed driving so she'd handed him her keys.

On the way, he made a sharp turn, and Holly grabbed for the door handle to steady herself. "Whoa." He pulled to a stop in a sea of cars—new cars, in a lot. "What happened?" The clock ticked on keeping the two men apart.

"I'm going to buy a car."

"Right this minute?" Maybe she needed to resign herself to the fact that these two men would be meeting each other. She had no relationship with Matt. For that matter, she wasn't certain of her relationship with Adam. She'd just started to feel like they had a deepening connection, then it had been blown apart. But he kept giving signals that he did want to be near her.

Yes, she did need to keep the two men apart. Jealous men did stupid things. A book she'd once read said that, and she'd found it to be quite true.

Adam, looking very much like a kid in a candy store, stepped out of her car. A saleswoman hurried over as Holly joined him. The woman gave Holly's car an expression of distaste, one that left Holly feeling like she should apologize for her car spending even this amount of time in the lot.

"Can I help you?"

"He wants to buy a car." Holly tapped Adam on the arm.

"It isn't for the two of you?"

"We aren't a couple. I'm his real estate agent. This is my car." Holly felt like she'd rushed the words.

"What can I help you with, sir?" The woman gave Adam a smile that could light up half the city—everything from downtown to Muldoon Road, maybe all the way to Eagle River.

Adam started toward a two-seater, red sports car. She thought it the perfect choice for him. Then he veered off and went toward the trucks. "Holly, you were in Dad's truck. Did you like it?"

He wanted her opinion on furniture *and* automobiles? That might be a good sign. "I thought it was nice that you could pack for an expedition with all that room—and still seat four people comfortably. The back seat was big enough that you could fit two people *and* Emma in there."

He grinned at her. "Emma loves riding in Dad's truck. She stands on the back seat and leans forward so she can see between the two front seats."

The saleswoman glanced from Adam to her and back, clearly uncertain about their dynamic, and wisely decided not to alienate anyone at this point. "If you're interested in that type of truck, we have a nice selection right now." They went to a section of the lot with the large vehicles lined up in rows and wandered between them. A dark silver caught her eye. When she stopped to read the sheet giving its specifications, Adam came up beside her.

He patted the side of the truck. "No moonroof."

"I'm not a fancy roof kind of girl, so that doesn't matter to me. I like the rest of it." She started to move on.

The saleswoman said, "We have that one with a moonroof." She pointed toward the end of the row and led the way over.

Holly, her eye on the clock, hurried over. Adam moved that direction but stopped to check out other trucks on his way.

At the new truck, Holly read the sheet. "Adam, this one is almost exactly the same. With your moonroof." She gave him an expression that showed him what she thought of his addition.

He grinned and stepped over to her. After reading the sheet, he walked around the truck. "It's the same model Dad owns, so I'm used to it. I like the color."

"Me too."

He turned to their representative. "I'll take it."

And with that, Adam bought a truck. She waited outside while he finished the transaction. When he came out, she gave him directions to the restaurant. Either Matt would come very late—always possible with him and his job—or their paths would cross. She voted for late and hoped none of her former feelings would taint what had been a pleasant day.

When Matt entered through the restaurant's doors and approached the hostess stand, Holly felt no attraction to him—no tingle of excitement at seeing her former beau. No regrets at not creating a future with him.

She did regret the fact that Adam still had a couple of bites of his salmon left. He'd eaten slowly and, twice during the meal he'd started to say something, but had cut himself off mid-sentence and said, "never mind." She'd tried to hustle him out the door when Matt texted ten minutes ago, using the excuse of the work he'd said he needed to do. He'd stayed, saying that he wanted to enjoy his meal. She'd certainly enjoyed hers . . . until that moment. She wouldn't find out what Adam had wanted to say now.

Adam's gaze followed hers. She knew he'd spotted Matt when he stilled, a forkful of salmon halfway to his mouth.

Adam gestured toward the other man. *"He's your client?"* He said every word slowly and deliberately.

She felt male jealousy coming on. "He wants to sell his house and buy a small condo."

"Shopping for a home can have an unexpected sense of intimacy to it. I know this personally."

Matt smiled at her when the hostess gestured toward their table. In the crowded restaurant, he may not have realized she wasn't alone. About six feet from their table, his eyes went from her to Adam and quickly back to her. He slowed his pace but continued. A twist near her heart told her she had a decision to make.

Adam abruptly set his fork on his plate, the metal clanking against the china. "I don't have any hold on you. You can, of course, have any client you choose."

"But you'd rather I didn't have this one."

"Yeah. But like I said, I don't have any hold on you."

With Matt a few feet away, she leaned closer to Adam. "Would it be better if I listed his house for sale—something that requires little time spent together—but had someone else take over his house hunt?"

"If you'd like."

"Adam, would you prefer that?"

"So much more." Adam pushed back his chair and stood, dropping his napkin beside his plate. Adam rested his hand on her shoulder. "Cooper. Good to see you." His tone said the opposite.

Not to be outdone in the male territory marking, Matt said, "You're beautiful as always, Holly."

"Thank you, Matt. Adam's just leaving. Why don't you take this empty chair?" Holly tapped the chair beside her at the table for four and Matt sat there. She watched Adam exit before turning her attention to the man beside her. She found him watching her.

"I thought he was a client."

"He is a client. I found a house for him." Matt clearly wanted her to elaborate, but she couldn't say what she still needed to sort out for herself. And she wouldn't have shared that piece of herself with him anyway.

"Matt, I'd like to sell your house for you." His smile told her he'd known she'd do that. "But I'm going to recommend two or three colleagues who could help you search for a new home."

His smile dropped. "You don't want to work with me? I thought it would be a way for us to spend time together."

"At our last meal in a restaurant, you made yourself clear. We had no future other than friendship. Or a one-night stand."

He broke eye contact. "More than one night. And looking back, I may have been hasty."

"I don't *feel* anything for you." She patted her chest. "Nothing in here."

Matt squirmed in his seat, probably something that would make the bad guys he'd arrested chuckle. "I understand. I wish I didn't, but I do. You want him." He pointed at the door Adam had left through.

Emotion rushed in—joy, contentment, excitement. "I believe I do. Can I list your house?"

At his nod, Holly brought her laptop out of her briefcase and booted it up.

Chapter Eighteen

Adam stood in his empty living room, studied his ever-growing to-do list, and made a note about painting the front door he'd come through moments ago. Any solid color would be an improvement over the chipped paint, but he leaned toward red.

After opening the windows facing the front to freshen the stale air in the formerly vacant house, he took in the scene in front of him and grinned like a kid who'd been given his first bicycle.

His feet itched to freely dance a jig through his living room—something he could do with style due to his grand-mother's teaching. She'd come to America from Ireland as a young woman and had said he needed to know his roots.

Holly's expected arrival made him re-evaluate. What would she think if she caught him dancing when she came to the door? Then again, she'd said she'd make a stop on the way to bring lunch to her girls over at Jemma's, where their aunt babysat them while she painted furniture.

Apparently, Jemma didn't put the right ratio of peanut butter and jelly on the bread. Until then, he hadn't realized anyone could mess up a peanut butter and jelly sandwich. Adam suspected it was just because she'd put it on a bagel. The woman loved bagels.

Bringing up a jaunty Irish tune on his phone, he hummed to the music for a moment, letting the rhythm settle in. He set his phone out of the way next to the wall and did a few warm-up steps. Once his feet were reacquainted with the dance, he took a few slow steps, then built faster and faster.

At age ten, he'd dreamed of dancing on stage. His wooden living room floor with the stunning view out the windows scored even higher than a professional stage to him. By the time the song ended, his calf muscles burned, and he could barely breathe. But he could feel his long-gone grandmother's presence in his new home.

Wincing when he took a step toward his phone, he knew that life had become too sedentary since the mess with his apartment. Swan Lake had given him sore muscles that lasted a week.

Slow clapping sounded from behind him. Wheeling around, he stared at Holly Harris who stood on the other side of one of the front windows.

"Amazing!" Abbie—who he'd started to be able to tell from her sister—said from beside her mother.

"Yes," her sister agreed.

"Impressive," Jemma added.

"You have hidden talents, Adam," Bree said. "Michael and I paid to see a show in New York with Irish dancing. You're just as good."

Two choices popped in front of him: be embarrassed or be funny. Humor won. "Thank you, dear ladies." With a wide sweep of his hand, he bent into a low bow.

The little girls giggled.

He danced a few more steps. "Would you like to see *my* house? I just love saying that."

Laughing, Holly opened the door, and they all entered.

Ivy ran up to him. "Can you teach us to dance?"

He couldn't imagine anyone not liking these little girls. Whether or not he taught one to dance though depended on his relationship with her mother. "Maybe some time."

Bree went straight through to the sliding glass doors. "You have a wonderful view. Michael and I do too, but ours is from above, and more like seeing a photo or a postcard. Standing here, I feel like I'm in a forest. Jemma and Nathaniel's place is like this."

"Exactly. Holly showed me their house so I could clarify what I wanted in mine. I knew I wanted that view for myself. But it made the house hunt a little harder."

Holly raised her eyebrows.

"More than a little?"

She seemed about to say something, then changed her mind. "I'm glad my client is happy."

Abbie tried one of the dance steps and did a passable job. Giving up on that, she asked, "Can we play with Emma?"

"I wanted to keep her safe while work was going on today, so she's at your Aunt Jemma's."

"I remember now. We played with her for a few minutes."

"I watched them," Jemma said before he could worry.

Turning his gaze to adult level again, he said, "As long as you're all here, please help me choose some paint colors."

Jemma visibly perked up at that.

"Follow me to my bedroom." He turned that way, immediately realizing how his words sounded. He was grateful he hadn't chosen the same words when he and Holly had been alone because she might have gotten the wrong idea. Well, not exactly wrong—but not appropriate. Looking back, he saw Bree and Jemma smile at each other. Holly wore a startled expression.

"Adam,"—Jemma asked, kindly changing the subject—"are you planning to remodel soon? Holly mentioned you'd be gutting your kitchen and starting over."

"No." Adam went up the stairs and entered his bedroom with the five females right behind him. "I realized it might be better to live in it for a while to know more clearly what I want to keep and the changes I'd like to make." He turned to see their expressions.

"There isn't anything unlivable about this house, unlike the one Michael bought before we married." Bree shuddered. "That wouldn't have worked, even in the short term."

Jemma turned in a slow circle. "Huge room, but it definitely needs a modern color palette. The woman of the house must have enjoyed mauve in the eighties." She and Bree stepped over to the master bathroom's doorway. "I'm not sure I've even seen a bathtub in that particular shade of pink before now."

"I wonder why any bathtub colors other than white are made," Bree said.

Jemma patted her sister on the shoulder. "So says a doctor who wants to know everything's clean."

"That tub will be one of my greatest challenges for living here. But I followed the old real estate saying: Location,

location, location. I can't make the view better, but I can make the house better. That tub will eventually go."

Holly picked up the stack of paint chips he'd set on the floor. "I like them all. I do love to paint."

Adam jumped on her words. "You actually like painting?"

"Oh, yeah. I find the repetitive motion almost relaxing. I've helped several clients paint after closing."

"She's a skilled painter," Jemma said. "And she's cheap to hire."

Holly held up her index finger. "Not always. I do expect to be fed when I paint."

He could have help, and not just any help but Holly's? "I'll get you whatever you want to eat if you paint."

"You could hire someone."

"I considered it, but it felt impersonal."

"Okay. I'll help you."

"Excellent. I'd like to do as much of the work in the house myself as I can." He paused. "Along with family and friends, of course."

Holly flipped through the paint chips. "I know you're a talented carpet cleaner, Adam, but this house is almost all hardwood floored, so your main skill won't be needed."

"Carpet cleaning skills? Please come to our house," Bree said. "A sandwich with raspberry jelly landed face down."

"We're still sorry about that, Aunt Bree," Ivy said.

"I know. But why did you open it up?"

Abbie sighed with a long-suffering tone well beyond her years. "We wanted to see what kind of jam was inside. Sometimes things don't taste the same at your house."

Holly chuckled.

Even Bree smiled at her niece's words. "Fair enough."

"They got you on that." Jemma chimed in. "Zucchini bread was a hit though. Just not the carrots in the scrambled eggs."

These sisters were a handful. Focusing on Holly, he walked over to stand behind her and looked over her shoulder at the paint chips she studied. "Which do you prefer?"

She frowned. "I don't think I should say. It's your room, Adam. What if the painter's taste isn't your taste?"

"What would you choose if you lived here? If this was your room?"

Hearing rustling sounds, he turned to discover Bree and Jemma ushering the girls out the door.

Holly followed his motions. "Hey!" she called after her family.

Someone closed the door.

Alone in his bedroom with Holly, even empty, didn't seem quite right. Respectable, sure, with chaperones just outside the door, but still . . . He took her hand in his and tugged her out onto the porch.

"Adam, I'm sorry about my sisters." Staring skyward, she whispered, "This is so embarrassing."

He turned her to face him. While he wouldn't have chosen this moment, he needed to know. Had he been a fool, or did she care for him? "I'm not sure where I stand with you. One minute I think we're a couple, the next minute I'm uncertain."

Holly looked up at him but didn't say anything.

"Do you feel *anything* for me other than gratitude for the sale?"

She stared at the paint chips in her hand.

Stepping back, he held up both hands. "I'm sorry. I assumed we were building a relationship. From your lack of comment, I can see it only exists in my mind." He reached for the handle of the door.

"Adam, wait!"

Still facing away from her, he said, "*Please* don't say we can still be friends."

"Look at me."

When he turned back, Holly stepped forward, wrapped her arms around him, and pulled him close.

"Holly?"

"Be quiet and kiss me."

He leaned down and did as asked, loving the feel of her arms around him. When she broke the kiss, he stood in a daze. "What just happened?"

"I had trouble saying the words." She hesitated for a few seconds before adding, "I believe I showed you I love you."

Adam's knees buckled, and he leaned against his house for support. "*Love* me?"

Holly looked up at the sky, then took another step back. "Did I move too fast?"

"No. I'm the happiest man there is. I love you too!" He wrapped his arms around her and held her close, the love he felt for this woman rushing through him. Releasing her, he gazed into her eyes and cupped her cheeks in his hands.

"I haven't told a man I loved him since my husband. It hasn't been easy for me to say those words, but I trust you with my heart, Adam. I'm sorry I didn't tell you about the girls earlier—"

"They're working their way into my heart."

She smiled widely. "I learned my lesson. I want to be honest about emotions and everything else. Secrets can destroy a relationship."

Oh no. He'd planned—over and over again he'd planned—to explain about his writing secret *before* they became serious. But leaving out that little piece of his life right now wouldn't be a problem, right? Not as long as he found a way to tell her soon.

"Thank you for loving me back." Holly put her hand on the side of his face and gently kissed him again.

He'd find a way to tell her tomorrow, when they were alone. And before she found out on her own. He glanced at the room through the open door. "Your sisters will probably ask which paint color you chose."

She burst into laughter and held up the chips. "They're still in my left hand." Flipping through them, she chose navy blue, handing it to him.

Adam went back into the room with Holly right behind him. Holding it up to the wall, he said, "Are you sure? I'd thought I might paint the kitchen cabinets this color."

"Ooh, I like that idea. So many men seem to be afraid of color." She went through the stack again. "I don't see what I'm picturing here instead of the navy." She looked up at him. "Maybe we could put a light taupe on the walls in this room, and accent with other soft colors like light blue or sage green?"

"Taupe?"

"It's kind of a beige. You should probably choose a color you can use in here and in the master bath, one that would be happy with your mauve bathtub."

"Agreed. Once the bathroom is remodeled, I may repaint, but it sounds livable."

A knock sounded on the bedroom door. "Um, we need to be on our way, Holly," Bree said softly.

"Come on in. We've decided on a paint color. I think." She looked up at him again.

"I'd draw the line at little girl pink, but other than that, I'm open. Oh, and roses. Definitely no roses."

"I like roses."

"I'll buy you vases of roses. Just please don't upholster with them or paste them on any walls with wallpaper."

Bree's gaze went from one to the other, as though she sensed a change.

"Ready?" Jemma peered around the corner. "Two little people are hungry," she said in a low voice.

"They get cranky when they're hungry," Holly said in that same tone. "We just don't mention it around them, because then they argue that they aren't cranky."

Jemma nodded. "It escalates from there."

Adam said, "Once the house cleaner Holly suggested does her job this afternoon, I'll feel better about putting food in the fridge and cupboards. The last owner seems to have left in a hurry." Remembering the house where Holly had dangled off the roof, he added, "But not in as big of a hurry as those clients of yours. Did that house sell yet?"

"There was a buyer, but their financing didn't come through. It's a nice house, too. Now that it's clean."

A small voice from the living room said, "No. I don't want to leave. I want to stay here with Adam." A small, dull sound after that made him wonder if a little foot had stomped the floor to punctuate those words.

"That's my cue." Holly handed the paint samples back to him.

"I guess I'll go buy paint once the cleaning lady gets going."

"I could probably come back today to paint, couldn't I, Jemma?"

A second small voice said, "Will Emma live here? I want to stay here too."

Holly gave him a sweet look then rushed toward the door.

Jemma glanced from her sister to him before answering. "Once they've eaten, peace will be restored. I would be happy to babysit. Right now, they're all yours, sister," she said as Holly passed her.

Returning to Adam's house a few hours later wearing paint-stained jeans, an old T-shirt, and sneakers that had seen better days, Holly fought against the silly grin that kept springing onto her face. Both Jemma and Bree had asked her about it. Even her girls had been giving her strange looks. But she wouldn't tell another soul until she'd had time to think about what had happened. Adam loved her and, she hoped, they'd have a future together. She felt connected to him in a way she'd never felt with Matt.

"I'm in love." She tried the words out loud. "I'm in love with Adam O'Connell." Joy rushed through her, and the grin grew wider.

She'd found a man she could trust. Both she and her girls deserved a man in their life who would be honest with them. A man with that quality wouldn't vanish. Everything was in the open now. He knew about her kids. He knew she dreamed of being a published author. He'd even met her parents. They'd had only good things to say about him, especially about the way he'd handled the canoe trip.

She pulled into Adam's driveway, then leaned over to check her appearance in the rearview mirror. Her hair had blown around her face in the wind from the open window, but maybe wild hair went with clothes spattered with every color she'd painted in the last five years. With the occasional day spent helping Jemma rehab furniture, along with walls in her own house, and those of friends and clients, she'd collected a spectacular array of colors.

After running her fingers through her hair, Holly got out of her car. Returning here felt somehow monumental, as though she was stepping into a new life.

Holly wanted to skip to the door, something her girls would giggle at, but she stayed dignified. At the door, she put her finger on the doorbell, then decided to peer through the window first.

When music had poured out of his windows earlier, she'd given a quick glance through one to find Adam performing his Irish dance. Now *that* had been a surprise. Chuckling, she found the room empty. Movement in the kitchen told her the cleaning woman was hard at work.

She rang the bell and heard footsteps approaching.

"Holly!" Adam opened the door and pulled her into a sweet hug, punctuated with a quick kiss. As he took her hand in his, she noticed his paint clothing: worn jeans paired with a faded flannel shirt. Instead of sloppy, he looked like an Alaskan man ready to take on the wilderness. Casual Alaska suited him.

Taking her hand, he led her through the room. "I've put down tarps and have all our painting gear ready." Up the stairs, they walked into the master bedroom, and she found a professional-looking scene. Canvas tarps covered the wood floors. He'd taped next to the windows on the sliding glass doors so they could easily paint the trim. And an open step ladder perched in the corner, waiting for him to paint the edges.

He explained the supplies before she could ask. "Dad surprised me by driving up this morning with the back of his truck full. Remember how I said he used to have rental properties?" At her nod, he continued, "We now have enough tarps to cover floors in several rooms at a time, two ladders, and all the paint rollers and brushes we could ever want."

Holly picked up a paint roller. Right now, she wanted a kiss more than she wanted to paint. What would he think if she asked? She'd kissed him earlier, but prancing into his house and demanding a kiss . . .

Begin a relationship as you mean for it to continue. She could hear her mother's words to her and her sisters as they grew up. Maybe Bree and Jemma had taken her advice. They'd certainly found men who loved and respected them.

"I believe I'd like a kiss before we begin the project." Holly's words reminded her of something Ivy would say. As she was about to rephrase it, Adam's arms wrapped around her. He lowered his head for a kiss that lasted longer, much longer, than the quick peck on the lips he'd given her before.

When he lifted his head, his expression looked just as dazed as she felt. "I think—" His voice broke. Clearing his throat, he said, "I think we should get to work."

Holly blew out a slow breath and touched her lips, which still tingled. "If we must."

He reached for her again.

She pointed to the can on the floor. "Paint?"

Adam chuckled as he knelt next to the paint can, and began working an opener around the edge of the lid. "Yes, ma'am." He popped off the lid, then lifted it to show her.

"This is the color I saw in my mind when you described taupe. I asked the man at the paint counter too."

"That's it! I know it will be a bit darker when it's dry, and that's good. Are you sure you'll like the color?"

"Are you kidding? After more than a month with my parents, I'm just happy it isn't pink."

"I have two little girls who adore pink and everything that's over-the-top girly. Lace and ribbons. Ruffles and bows." His eyes widened as her list grew. "I'm used to pink."

"I've been in your house, and your living room doesn't have any of that. You saw my parents' house. There's pink, floral wallpaper in the kitchen."

Her lips twitched as she remembered that room. "Only my girls' bedroom is over-the-top feminine."

"That makes your house livable. Let's paint this first." He pointed at the large wall one saw when entering the room. "The bed is scheduled to arrive today, and I think against that wall is the best place for it. I'd like to have the wall dry by then."

"No problem with that. It's probably in the seventies, and with low humidity. We may have two coats on the walls by then."

He poured paint into the roller pan. "How fast of a painter are you?"

"I've knocked out a room this size in an afternoon by myself. We'll make it. We can move on to another room then if you have more paint."

Holly rolled paint on the walls while Adam cut in the edges. In an hour, they'd finished the first coat. It dried so quickly that they started on a second coat over the same path as the first and finished it.

When the doorbell rang as Adam painted the door's creamy-white trim, he checked his watch. "The bed is supposed to arrive in an hour." He stepped out the door and rushed back in. "I can see the delivery truck in the driveway. They're here early." When he reached for a paint can, Holly pushed him toward the door.

"You let them in. I'll start the cleanup." She set the paint cans and painting equipment on the deck outside, being careful not to touch the half-painted door trim. Then she folded up the tarps and stacked them in the corner of the room. When she carefully touched the paint on the wall the bed would rest against, her finger came back dry.

The delivery team first brought in a metal frame they assembled, then the box spring, and finally the mattress—unwrapping a cover of plastic around each of the last two. When they left minutes later after a whirlwind of activity, a large—very large—bed had the place of honor in the room.

"Is it just me," she asked Adam once he'd followed the men to the door and returned, "or does that seem to be the largest bed you've ever seen?"

He chuckled. "That it does."

"It feels improper, for lack of a better word, for me to be in here now. And that's silly."

"I love your honesty. And you're right. It feels the same way to me. Let me finish the trim. Then we can take inventory of the rest of the house." He glanced around the room. "Where's the—" He apparently spotted the painting gear outside, because he headed that direction. She spread out a tarp then followed after him, helping him bring everything back inside.

"While you finish here, I'll check on the cleaning."

He gave a nod as he carefully wielded the brush on the door trim. "I'll meet you in the great room when I'm done."

Downstairs, she found the cleaning woman finishing the powder room, its fixtures a much brighter shade of gold. Holly stepped away and went into the kitchen, a room transformed through skilled cleaning. The cupboards appeared newer, so she must have taken them on. Out of the corner of her eye, Holly saw her moving around in the great room.

When the woman began gathering her things, Holly approached her. "Done?"

"Yes. Mr. O'Connell already paid me."

"You did a great job. I'll keep recommending you to clients."

The woman smiled. "Thank you. I'll clean your house anytime you want as a thank you."

Holly helped her carry her gear out, then returned to the great room. Waiting for Adam, she tapped her foot and tried to picture the room with a fresh coat of paint. She moved over to the kitchen's doorway and considered different ways to freshen it up.

Checking her phone, she saw that only ten minutes had passed, but it felt like at least an hour. Doing nothing wasn't her specialty. She thought of Adam as he finished up painting. A room with a bare mattress wouldn't work for tonight. She called upstairs. "Adam, I can make the bed. Where are the sheets and blankets?"

He appeared at the top of the stairs with the brush in his hand. "I keep forgetting that I no longer have those basics. I had 'buy a bed' in mind—not 'buy a bed and everything that goes on it.'"

"Your first night isn't going to be very comfortable if we don't buy those things." As soon as the words left her mouth, she wanted to take them back. "I should have said that *you* can buy them. I became a little too involved for a minute." She laughed in a way that, to her ears, sounded forced.

Adam disappeared for a moment, then returned without the paint brush. She could almost see his mind whirring as he came down the stairs, his expression becoming more and more determined. He headed straight for her and gave her a quick kiss. "You're part of my life now. *We* are what I want."

"We're a couple." She tested the words and liked the sound of them. "I don't give my trust easily, but you've earned that and my respect."

Emotions streamed across his face, ranging from concern to panic, and stopping there.

"Is anything wrong?"

"Wrong? No, of course not. Everything's great."

"Would you like to run to the store now?"

He checked his watch. "One other delivery is scheduled for today—a desk for my office. They should be here within the hour." He took her hand in his and held it, the warmth shooting right to her heart. Everything felt *right* with him. "Help me choose the other colors for the house. I want your input in everything."

That sounded like more than a little commitment. But delving into her feelings about a permanent relationship should be left to a solitary moment. Shaking that off, she considered his words. Picking paint colors sounded fun. She had started to see why Jemma enjoyed decorating. "Are you planning to knock down the wall between the kitchen and the dining area, as I suggested?"

"Eventually. I liked all of your suggestions."

"These are big rooms to paint. When does the other furniture arrive?"

"I thought I was going to have to paint by myself, so I didn't schedule any other deliveries until next week. The bed and desk were planned for today so I could sleep and work."

"I'm surprised there isn't a van filled with comfortable couches and a big-screen TV at the curb right now."

"I did buy the big-screen TV," Adam added with an adorable little-boy-at-Christmas expression. "But I knew I wouldn't want to move it to paint. Delivery is next week for that too."

They went from room to room, deciding to use cream in the upstairs living room along with an undecided accent wall. He chose a lavender blue for the guest room, with his mother in mind. He said he wanted his parents to always feel comfortable staying overnight in the big city, but couldn't go as far as pink. The doorbell rang while they were standing in that room, and they hurried downstairs.

Once the delivery crew had the desk tucked into Adam's small office behind the stairs, they left to buy bed furnishings for Adam's bed. If that didn't feel intimate, she didn't know what would.

At Adam's, after their shopping spree, she helped him unload his purchases, receiving a sweet kiss for her efforts. Then she headed toward Jemma's house and her kids. Her parents' RV in the driveway surprised her but told her the part they'd needed must have arrived. Stepping from her car, she heard happy, childish squeals from the backyard and then a bark. Chloe must be visiting. That meant tired girls—

something she would normally be grateful for at the end of the day. But she was tired too.

"Mommy, Mommy." Abbie rushed over to her. "We went for a walk with Chloe."

"Yes, a long walk," Ivy added, then yawned.

Her dad came around the corner of the house. "We saw you pull up. We're making our annual salmon dinner tonight with what we caught yesterday. Your sisters and their husbands will be here. Would you like to invite Adam?" His tone of voice told her he was fishing for information with as much interest as he had for the salmon.

After orchestrating their canoe trip, she wasn't sure she wanted her parents involved in her dating life. But that trip had been a turning point for her relationship with Adam. Maybe she owed them some thanks. On second thought, Jemma had just begun dating Nathaniel last summer when he'd been invited, and she'd later compared the dinner to the Inquisition.

"Maybe next time." At her dad's disappointed expression, she changed subjects. "Will you be going fishing for halibut?" She adored the creamy, white meat of halibut.

"Of course."

Her mother stepped out the back door. "How was the canoe trip?"

Both were fishing, this time for information, but she refused to take the bait.

"Wet. Very, very wet."

Her parents looked at each other, and her mother gave a slight shake of her head, warning her father not to push if Holly had to venture a guess. The girls ran circles around the yard with Chloe, making it difficult to tell who was chasing who.

"Would you mind if we borrowed your girls again tomorrow? We're going up to Hatcher Pass for a picnic. Nathaniel is loaning us his SUV, so we don't have to take our giant vehicle on the winding gravel roads up there."

She hadn't wanted them to go overnight again for a while but didn't feel right standing in the way of a day trip. "You'd leave in the morning?"

"Of course," her mother said slowly. "Unless that's a problem."

"Abbie and Ivy love it up there. I'll have them ready right after breakfast."

Chapter Nineteen

On the way to Adam's the next morning, Holly wondered if she should have tried to talk to her girls about her and Adam becoming closer. Putting it off didn't seem wise. Maybe they'd have enough energy left tonight for a chat.

Right, and maybe pigs could fly. After running around outside, they always came back excited then fell asleep.

She had thought business commitments would keep her away from Adam's today, but her uncertain client had canceled her showings. Holly had been right about the woman because she'd decided to stay where she was and continue renting. At least they wouldn't waste more time on a fruitless search. She'd called Adam to let him know his free help would arrive soon.

When she turned onto his street, a thrill shot through Holly. A day had passed since their relationship had deepened. Maybe he'd reconsidered his words. Pulling into his driveway, she willed her heartbeat to slow down. No, he'd been clear about loving her. It hadn't seemed spur of the moment or part of the rush of moving into his first house. *Adam loved her.*

She stepped out of her car and made her way up the walk. They'd already improved the inside of the house, but the house's drab exterior needed a facelift just as much. Planting a row of flowers, reseeding the lawn, maybe adding another tree—those changes would make the house more inviting. Adam could probably afford to do all of those things now.

He seemed to have a higher-than-average income. She'd heard that professors had incomes similar to other teachers, so not as well paid as many other professions, but Adam had paid cash for his house. His parents lived in a nice, comfortable house, but it wasn't fancy, so she doubted he'd been born with overflowing cash. Maybe he'd received an inheritance as she and Jemma had.

At the front door, she reached for the doorbell, then changed her mind and tried the doorknob. When it turned, she opened the door and called out. "Adam, are you home?"

"Just a sec." He called from off to the right, she guessed from his office. Professors must work, even during summer break. He gave her a big smile as he walked into the room. When he reached Holly, he wrapped his arms around her, pulled her close, then dropped a kiss on her mouth. "I'm glad you're here. It seems we're both dressed for work." He gestured toward her clothes that now sported the addition of taupe paint. "I thought we'd get everything taped and prepped for painting, then begin painting downstairs."

Holly took in the great room, an area she enjoyed more each time she saw it. A stack of tarps filled the corner of the room. "Sounds like a plan. I'll prepare the kitchen."

"Okay. I'll go upstairs. It won't take me long to slap a coat of paint on the hall bath. It needs a major update, but paint should help."

"Are you using cream there?"

He nodded. "I thought neutral might help tone down the orange tile."

She laughed. "It isn't exactly orange. I'd say it's more of a rust."

"Well, since rust is on things that are old, I'll join you in that description." He picked up a tarp and a paint can before heading upstairs.

Holly took a roll of tape and went toward the kitchen. Then she veered to the right. The kitchen would take an hour to prep. She'd start with his office. They could finish it quickly and feel like they'd accomplished something before tackling the larger jobs.

Entering the room for the first time since their initial house tour, she found a glass-topped desk with a laptop open on it. He had set it up in the middle of the room, she guessed temporarily, so painting around it would be easier. Unfolding the tarp, she threw it over the desk and began draping it over the top of the computer and a stack of books. Noticing the blinking cursor on a word processing app caused her to stop before she let go of it.

She pushed the tarp back a bit and glanced at the door. Would Adam mind if she read the document? He'd read a lot of her writing. She'd probably be bored out of her mind with a scholarly article on Shakespeare, or a lengthy instruction on teaching writing to freshmen. Holly sat down and checked it out. He was on page 203 of a document. Did professors write anything that long after graduating from college?

She began reading. In a few lines, she realized that a science fiction novel filled the screen. The stack of books on the desk took on a new light. Also science fiction, these were all by the same author, an A. T. Martin. She flipped to the back of one. There wasn't an author photo, but she did read the book's description. The main character had the same name as a character on the computer's screen. Randomly opening the book, she read a page, then chose another. The writing style was the same.

Adam O'Connell wrote science fiction novels under the name A. T. Martin. How exciting! He was a successful novelist. That must have been where he'd gotten the money to buy his house. But that would mean he'd sold a whole lot of books. She didn't read science fiction, so she'd never heard of him. A quick check on a major bookselling site showed her his books were highly rated and had a bunch of reviews. He appeared to be super successful.

He hadn't mentioned this major part of his life to her. Holly jumped to her feet, wobbling as she did. That meant he didn't trust her.

She'd trusted him. Yes, she hadn't told him about her girls, but they'd barely started dating then. Yesterday, they'd talked about honesty. Racing out of the room, she stood at the bottom of the stairs. "Adam O'Connell!"

He came to the top with the roll of tape in his hands. "Yes? Is something wrong?" He started down the stairs, stopping halfway down. "Is everything okay?"

"I thought I'd get a smaller room prepped first." She stabbed a finger toward his office. "Why didn't you tell me?"

Silence greeted her.

The anger evaporated and tears built in her eyes, one drop falling as she waited for his reply. She swiped it away as the silence continued. "Never mind." At that, she grabbed her purse and slammed the door behind her with everything she had.

Driving from Adam's house in Chugiak to hers in Palmer, Holly felt a pie baking event coming on. Wiping tears from her cheeks, she focused on the road the best she could through the sheen. She needed to bake a pie or two or three today to calm down. To focus.

Stopping at the first grocery store she came to in Palmer, she fought for enough control to be able to buy what she needed—flour, butter, shortening, fruit, milk, cream, and anything else that sounded pie-worthy today—without being fitted for a straitjacket by a well-meaning store clerk. She smiled at a former client who exited the store as she entered. Fortunately, the man seemed to be in a hurry, so they exchanged nothing more than a greeting.

As she filled a produce bag with apples, she willed herself to focus on the positive. She had her girls. Every man she'd been serious about had disappointed her, but her family always loved her. Taking a big breath, she let it out slowly.

Moving through the store at a pace just under a run, she soon finished, topping her cart off with a few cans of soup, some bread, and cheese—everything she'd need for a soup and sandwich dinner. Anything more complicated would probably be beyond her by then. And her girls did deserve to eat something more than their weight in pie.

With the goods paid for, she wheeled everything to her car, squeezed it all into the trunk, and headed for home. The phone rang on the way, but when she saw Adam's photo on the screen, she ignored the call—along with the next three calls he made to her.

By mid-afternoon, her stress level had dropped from skyscraper to near ground level. She lifted a thin sliver out of an apple pie with a crumb topping and sampled it. The sugar-to-apple tartness ratio tasted right. When the cinnamon-spiced fruit melted on her tongue, she remembered the last time she'd made a pie with apples. Adam had stopped by. No danger of that today.

With that thought, the tears she'd successfully dammed up the last few hours burst forth, streaming down her cheeks as she stood at the stove stirring the vanilla filling for a graham cracker crust pie. Brushing tears away with the back of her hand, she watched the mixture thicken, took it off the burner to cool, then began slicing the bananas she'd arrange on the crust.

A knock at her front door made her jump. *Adam better not be out there.* She'd give him a piece of her mind, and in her present condition, that might be something he wouldn't forget. Peering out the curtain, she saw both of her sisters standing on her stoop. When she opened the door, they rushed inside and gathered her close.

"We're sorry," Jemma said.

"How did you know?" Holly asked cautiously. She hadn't told them, so who?

Jemma answered the mystery with a mystery. "Adam called and said you needed us."

"Why would he do that?" The buzzer sounded on her peach pie, so she ushered them inside and hurried into the kitchen. After checking the pie for doneness, she set the timer for another few minutes.

Jemma and Bree stared at her kitchen peninsula.

"Are you going into business?" Bree asked.

"No." Pies sat crust to crust across the granite surface. Holly counted the desserts. Nine. Maybe she had gone a little overboard. "I had to bake out some stress."

Bree waved a hand toward the counter. "Some? There are a lot of restaurants that don't serve this much dessert in a week."

"I guess we should be glad she didn't make cream pies too," Jemma pointed out. "Remember the time she broke up in high school and made five cream pies? We ate pie for a week."

Bree nodded. "And gave away a banana and a coconut cream."

Holly pulled open the door of her fridge. Another of the coconut-chocolate pies nestled against two other pies. The next shelf was equally crowded. The timer went off again, and this time the peach-filled confection was ready.

As she set it on a cooling rack, Bree said, "Let's sit down and talk."

Holly did as was asked, with Bree on one side and Jemma on the other.

"Holly, Adam told us what he did. He called Bree and me."

"And he's sorry, right?" Holly fell back against the cushions with her arms crossed. "He could have told me about his books a hundred times, but he didn't trust me with his secret."

Jemma silently watched her. "You're right."

"I am?"

"Absolutely. But that doesn't mean you shouldn't accept his apology."

"I *need* to trust the man in my life. I don't want any more secrets."

Jemma muttered, "Like a secret wedding, right?"

Bree stepped into the conversation, wisely ignoring the comment about her wedding. "Do you love Adam?"

Holly sniffed and nodded.

Jemma said, "Then what are you doing? At least listen to the man's explanation. He said that he'd wanted to tell you about his writing early on, but he didn't feel like he knew you well enough. It's a closely-held secret. Then every time he planned to tell you, something would come up. He'd planned to do it the day you went furniture shopping, but Matt walked into the restaurant."

Holly remembered that he had seemed about to say something.

"But what about all the other times we've been together? What about yesterday?"

"There's no question about it. The man made a mistake. Maybe let him grovel a little."

"Grovel?"

"Yes, Nathaniel grovels well when he goofs. I didn't tell anyone else when he forgot my birthday. He groveled big time for that. He made my favorite foods for three days."

Holly felt the first smile on her face since that morning. "How can I trust him again?"

"Did he cheat on you with another woman? Serve time for a drug conviction? Have a secret child?"

"No. But I *feel* betrayed."

Bree said, "Maybe like when he learned you had two children? But he took the news gracefully and accepted them?"

Holly thought about that day. He could have yelled or quietly walked away. He could have torn out of there on his motorcycle. He'd even told her that the girls were working their way into his heart. "I do see your point." She pursed her lips. "Do you think I overreacted?"

Bree added, "You'll have to figure that out."

"Let him win me back?"

Jemma reached her arm around Holly's shoulders and gave her a squeeze. "I say, yes. If you want him back."

She considered the situation. Life with Adam had been so much better than life without. Holly, feeling like life might be okay after all, rose to her feet. "Maybe he will think twice about keeping secrets in the future."

"I'd bet on it," Bree said as she stood. "Will you be okay alone?"

"I'm fine now." Holly turned to her kitchen. "I may have more pie than we can eat though."

"You think so?" Jemma laughed, also rising to her feet.

The three of them studied the counter.

Bree offered the solution. "A patient told me about a homeless shelter in Anchorage. I helped them serve lunch one day last week, and am certain they'd take these off your hands."

"Thank you! Let's pack them up." She pulled a roll of foil out of the cupboard. "All except the banana cream. You know how much the girls love that."

By the time they'd loaded up Bree's back seat, passenger seat, and trunk with pies, and she'd watched both sisters drive away, Holly felt better.

Adam pulled into her driveway before they were out of sight. She wondered if he'd been waiting and watching, hoping they'd help his cause. He jumped out of his car as soon as he came to a stop. "Holly, please forgive me."

"We've both made mistakes." She knew he wasn't her first husband, and he wasn't Matt.

"I love you, Holly Harris. Please forgive me."

"Adam, I promise to never keep secrets from you again. I mean, other than Christmas presents or something like that. Can you promise to never keep secrets?"

"I do."

Epilogue

"I do." Adam answered the minister's question.

"Do you, Holly Harris, take this man, Adam O'Connell, to be to your lawfully wedded husband?"

"I do."

"Then, by the powers vested in me by the state of Alaska, I now pronounce you husband and wife. You may kiss the bride."

When they kissed, the joy of the moment brought back the night in September when he'd proposed.

She'd asked the man kneeling in front of her, "When do you want to get married?"

"I don't want to wait too long."

"Maybe Christmastime? Both you and my dad are on a school break then. And my birthday's on Christmas Eve."

Adam glanced up at her. "That's why they named you Holly?"

She nodded. "Mom's always joked that it was better than Tinsel."

Adam stood. "We could get married two days before Christmas. We'll celebrate your birthday and the holiday somewhere special. Tropical or snowy?"

"Tropical."

"I like that idea. You won't need all those layers of clothes then."

She rolled her eyes. "Men."

"I think we just planned a wedding."

When the newly married couple turned from the minister to the group gathered here today, relief flooded through her at the large number of family and friends who'd chosen to come to their wedding. Nerves had blinded her to everyone in the church on her way up the aisle. It seemed that those who'd said they would come had, despite the four inches of snow they'd received overnight. To an Alaskan, that wasn't much more than a light dusting, but she'd still wondered if it would deter some of their guests.

She'd invited Matt Cooper and his sister Cathy. He'd declined, but Pete and Cathy McCormick, married earlier than they'd originally planned, sat on the bride's side of the church. She was glad to hold onto Cathy's friendship even without Matt in her life. The soon-to-be married Leah Kinkaid and Ben Shepherd sat behind them. They would be married January third, on the same day his grandparents had tied the knot.

When Holly stood at the back of the church, ready to walk up the aisle earlier, the church lights were dimmed. Dozens of white candles lit her path and glowed nearby. She'd chosen a snow-white wedding gown sprinkled with crystals that now sparkled in the candlelight. Adam looked amazing in a black tuxedo, white shirt, and black bow tie.

Jemma stood beside Holly, stunning in a silver gown even though, or maybe especially because, she was just two months from delivering Holly's first niece. Sure, she knew that men determined the sex of the child, but girls did seem to run in the family. Bree, standing beside her in a shimmering, gold dress to coordinate with her coloring, had learned only a week ago that she'd be having a baby next summer.

Two of Adam's brothers were positioned at his side, the other two beside his parents in the pew. She'd met all but one of his brothers a few months ago, and the other one this week. They were a family of five handsome, nice men, and he was the first to marry. She might have to help with that.

Abbie and Ivy, dressed in matching green, velvet dresses, had sprinkled white rose petals down the aisle, then taken their places with their grandparents on one side and their great-grandparents on their other.

Grandma Eleanor gave a wave just for her eyes, and Holly grinned. The older woman had found a new life with her new husband. So many things had changed for the Harris family in less than two years.

Adam looped her arm through his, and they stepped down the three steps to the church aisle. Moving forward, Holly wanted to pinch herself. She saw Adam catch his brother Mark's eye and grin. They were closest in age, and she could tell he felt closest to him.

His dad wore a suit, something he apparently didn't enjoy from the way he ran his fingers around the neck of his dress shirt every few minutes—but Adam had warned her about that. *Find a way to get him to take off the suit coat and tie as soon as possible*, he'd requested. And she would when they arrived at the reception. His mother wore a floral print dress. No surprise there. She'd spent a lot of time with Adam's parents, and his mother did love flowers on anything and everything.

Adam had helped her finish her book, and it was now for sale online. Every copy sold brought a smile to her face because someone wanted to read what she wrote. She wasn't in Adam's league yet, but she planned to get there.

Together, they walked down the aisle past their family and friends, toward their new life.

Dear Readers,

I want to thank you for reading *Crazy About Alaska* and hope you enjoyed Holly and Adam's story. If you did, please give a review on your favorite bookseller's site or Goodreads. Much of what happens in an author's world depends on the number of positive reviews.

At CathrynBrown.com, you will be able to keep up with what's happening in the series. Pete and Cathy's story is told in *Together in Alaska,* a short story I give as a thank you gift to those who sign up for my newsletter.

If you found the series with this book, you'll want to go back to the beginning and see what you missed. Jemma and Nathaniel's story is *Falling for Alaska.* There's a Christmas novella, *Merrying in Alaska,* and a spin-off series about Adam's brothers that begins with *Accidentally Matched.*

As with the other books, I take you places I've been. I camped in the exact spot where Adam, Holly, and her girls did on the Swan Lake Canoe Route. Drizzle dampened that weekend but didn't rain us out.

My family owned a plane, and I learned to fly. I flew over the same places Adam did. I've landed at Birchwood Airport, the one near his new house. I've also flown to Kenai.

I'd caught very few salmon until I discovered dipnetting. Standing in a fast-moving river and having the salmon bump into you is an amazing feeling.

Thank you again for spending time with Holly and Adam!

If you began the Alaska Dream Romance series
with this book, enjoy this sneak peek at
the first book in the series

Falling for Alaska

Falling for Alaska
Chapter One

"Bench or bookshelf? Which do you want to be?" Jemma Harris walked around the beat-up old dresser sitting in the garage next to the house her great-aunt had recently left her in Palmer, Alaska. She removed the drawers and stepped back. Nodding once, she said, "Bench." Jigsaw in hand, Jemma began the transformation.

Out of the corner of her eye, she saw Mr. Gorgeous from across the street open his front door. He wore his usual neatly pressed chinos and dress shirt, his dark, wavy hair adding the only element slightly out of control. Refocusing on the blade in her hand, Jemma cut off the dresser's top, then started a curve on the right side.

Something poked her shoulder. When she reached out to brush it away, her hand met with warm skin. Jumping backward, Jemma stood with the jigsaw in front of her like a weapon.

"What are you doing?" Mr. Gorgeous shouted over the sound of the saw.

Gorgeous but none too bright. She pushed the off switch and removed her protective glasses. "I'm sawing wood."

"No." He sighed with obvious frustration. "What are you doing making so much noise?"

"Um, creating a bench?" She pointed at the half-altered dresser. Seeing it in her mind in a fresh yellow with white trim and a matching padded seat, she knew it would be beautiful. "A parent will happily buy it for their daughter's room—at least I hope so."

Her neighbor's mouth dropped open. "This is a business? The noise I've put up with for weeks isn't temporary?"

"Yes. No. Yes, I'm planning to open a store."

"So you won't continue making noise here and being a general nuisance?"

Now he had her hackles up. "A nuisance?"

His hand swept over the area. "Noise. Grime. Chaos."

Focus on patience. He was her neighbor, so they needed to get along. Forcing a calm note to her voice, she said, "I'm Jemma Harris. It may appear chaotic to you, Mr. . . . ?"

"Nathaniel Montgomery."

"But I can assure you everything is under control."

With a little too much eagerness, he asked, "Will you be gone soon?"

As soon as I can make this pay, she thought, wondering how someone so attractive on the outside could be the opposite on the inside.

Ready to ask him to leave, Jemma saw a truck come around the bend of the road and pull into her driveway, saving her from herself. Wondering who could be visiting when she'd lived in Palmer all of three weeks and hardly knew a soul, she noticed the load in the back. Travis, the man she'd met at the community yard sale and hired to deliver goods for her, was here, and his truck was filled to the brim with what she knew were great things. When she ventured a glance at her neighbor, his expression said otherwise.

Travis stepped out of his truck. "My sister had a few things left from her yard sale. I added the ones I thought you might want." He pointed at the back of his truck toward several items she hadn't bought.

Jemma climbed onto the side to see better. "Thank you, Travis. The bench and stool are great." She pushed a music stand aside. "And that lamp. What's in the box up there?" She pointed past the dresser, headboard, and coffee table she'd bought to right behind the cab of the truck.

"Some old tablecloths. Maybe some old fabric too. My mother doesn't even remember who gave them to her. She had the box stored in a closet, and no one at the sale wanted it, so she told me to throw it away. I thought I'd see if you wanted any of it."

How had she missed that at the sale? Jemma swallowed and tried for a nonchalant appearance so he wouldn't know how much she loved old linens and up the amount he wanted. As she scrambled into the back of the truck and over furniture, she realized she might have spoiled her attempt. When she reached the box, she folded back the flaps—and discovered a treasure trove of tablecloths from the 1940s and 1950s. "I can take these off your hands." She gulped. "At the right price."

"Just take them. Mom will be happy someone wants them."

She added extra to the amount she paid for the other goods. Jemma knew she'd gotten a good deal and from the expression on Travis's face, it looked like he thought he'd gotten a good deal too. That was how she always hoped to do business.

By the time Travis drove off, Nathaniel was standing with his mouth hanging open. "But that's junk! You paid for junk!"

"No, I paid for things I can revamp into products I can sell. This isn't junk." She picked up the lamp that had a shredded shade over a black-and-gold base from another, perhaps less appealing, era. "Well"—she shrugged—"some of it might be junk *now*, but everything will be beautiful when I'm done with it."

Nathaniel leaned over her pile of goods and nudged the stool with his foot. "I know I wouldn't want any of it. This just solidifies what I said earlier. I've put up with the noise for two weeks, and now we have truckloads of junk dropping by. This business," he said in the same tone she'd use to describe smelly garbage, "must be against the law."

"Mr. Montgomery—"

"Nathaniel."

They definitely were not on a first-name basis. "Mr. Montgomery, my business complies with all laws and codes. In short, it's legal."

His cell phone rang as Jemma inhaled, ready to impale him with her words. Speaking into the phone, he crossed the street to his house. About halfway, he gave a halfhearted wave in her general direction.

That was that, Jemma thought. It was probably best that he'd left because she didn't like the way she had been about to act. Nathaniel Montgomery seemed to bring out the worst in her.

Her sister Holly's silver compact came into sight about the same time he reached his front steps. Jemma's nieces waved out the window, bringing sunshine that helped clear out the Nathaniel Montgomery storm.

"Hi, Aunt Jemma!" Abbie shouted out the window.

"Me too!" Ivy added.

When the car stopped, Jemma pulled open a door and helped unbuckle the four-year-old twins from their car seats. As they climbed out, their mother directed them to the old swing set in the backyard, the same one she and Jemma had used as children when their family visited Great-aunt Grace.

"I noticed Mr. Gorgeous going into his house," Holly said. "Did you get to meet him? Is he as swoon-worthy up close as he is from a distance?"

"Yes. And n-o."

Holly's brow furrowed. "What's yes?"

"I met Mr. High and Mighty."

Her sister winced.

"And I've brought chaos into this neighborhood."

"Great-aunt Grace sold him land to build his house, and the other thirty acres to a builder for the subdivision around the corner—but on the other side of the woods. You and he *are* 'the neighborhood.'"

"And I've apparently ruined it with my sawing, junk deliveries, and general sense of chaos."

"I think I'm speechless, and I didn't know that could happen." Holly glanced at her watch. "I'd like to hear more, but I have to get to my job interview. If I don't find something soon, I'm going to have to get a job in another field. Wish me the best, and thanks for watching the kids."

"You're a great teacher, and you'll land a job soon, Holly. You graduated less than a month ago, so *don't* worry. And you know I'm always happy to watch the girls. I didn't get to spend much time with them before I moved here, but I can make up for that now." Just then, the furniture in her driveway caught Jemma's eye. "Hey, Holly. If you have a minute to spare, give me a hand getting this dresser into the garage."

Her sister grabbed one end, Jemma the other; then they hoisted the dresser off the ground and shuffled it into the open garage, setting it on the sawdust-covered, concrete floor.

Looking up, Holly reached over and pushed on one of the garage's loose wall boards. "This building is a little rickety."

"It's solid. It's just old." Jemma brushed off her shirt front.

"Speaking of old, you seem to really be getting into your new vintage fashion look." Holly raised one eyebrow.

"I'm thrilled to be able to wear whatever I want, to not adhere to the company's business conservative dress code. Suit. Closed-toe shoes. Stockings." Jemma shuddered. Glancing down at the hippie-ish peasant top she'd tucked into 1970s-era high-waisted jeans, Jemma asked, "Do you think it's too much?"

"It's . . . unique." Then, shaking her head, Holly said, "I'm off."

Jemma followed her sister back outside, then stood with Abbie and Ivy at her side as Holly climbed back into her little car and drove away. When she asked her nieces, "Would you like to sew later?" they gave an enthusiastic reply of "Yes!" Laughing, she picked up the box of linens and set them inside the front door.

When she came out, the girls were chasing each other around the garage. Jemma spoke above their happy-at-play sounds, "Stay in sight of the garage's back door, and I'll work for a little longer." She heard squealing as she went back in and settled into her work.

Glancing up every couple of minutes, she kept an eye on her nieces while she finished sawing the arms of the bench. Finishing this piece of furniture kept her complying with her plan. She would make this business a success.

Before Jemma began sanding, she stepped out the door and found the girls swinging. Happy to find them having fun, she went back into the garage. Back at work, she gave an initial sanding to the arms and back edge of her bench, then switched to a finer grit to give the whole piece a once-over. After brushing on a coat of white paint—she'd re-coat it later today and add the trim—she checked her watch and knew she'd better sew with the girls, or it would be too late.

"Girls!" She waved them over. "Ready to make something fun?"

When they stepped into the entry and Abbie saw the box of fabric, she shrieked with glee. Jemma knelt beside her and went through the box with the little girl, who cared as much about it as she did, while Ivy happily played with Stitches, the cat Jemma babysat for her other sister, Bree.

Jemma hoped she'd have a little girl just like one of her nieces. Someday when she wasn't so busy with life. Of course, she'd first want a man who loved her for who she was, not someone like Mr. Montgomery, who wanted everyone to conform to his rules.

Nathaniel set his phone on his desk and stared down at his neighbor's property from his office window. When he'd bought land across the street from a sweet old lady with a house as old as she was, surrounded by a white picket fence, he figured this would be a quiet place to live, a change from the condo he'd owned in downtown Anchorage. The old lady was gone, Jemma Harris had inherited, and she might be cute at first glance, with her long, blonde hair, big blue eyes and slender figure, but she was chaos through and through.

He should probably try to get along with her, and he would try to be neighborly. Her apparent love of garage sale finds even made her clothing chaotic, the different eras clashing loudly. Pushing off from the window, he chuckled to himself. As a marketing consultant, he'd learned a little bit about a lot of things, including fashion and football. He'd admit to the second but never the first.

A shriek pierced the air. He started to run for the stairs, but when a second shriek sounded, he realized the sound came from a child at play. Back at the window, he saw two identical little girls running around the front lawn of his neighbor's house. Great: sawing, hammering, and screaming. What more could one ask for during his workday?

Reaching for his phone, he scrolled down, found the number of his lawyer, and called. After a brief but odd delay, during which he heard the secretary pushing buttons on the phone, she came back and said she would try again. Moments later his lawyer came on the phone. Nathaniel asked, "Pete, do you have a minute?" The other man answered that he did, so Nathaniel outlined the situation with his neighbor.

When Pete said, "I'll check into it," Nathaniel asked, "That's it? No, 'I'll get an injunction' or some other legal-sounding answer?"

"I'll give you a shout when I know more later today. I'd ask if you'd like to shoot some hoops later, but I have a brief to finish and will probably be here late."

Nathaniel would have bowed out of it anyway. He'd given in after a string of requests last year and played basketball with some of the guys he did business with in town. Now they all assumed he'd want to do it again. He hadn't had anyone close enough to be a friend since middle school and didn't see that changing anytime soon. "Thanks. If anyone can help, I know you can."

When he'd hung up, he put on one of Mozart's flute concertos and felt the soothing music calm him. Good thing, because when he checked his e-mail, Nathaniel discovered a mess he had to sort out for a client. He loved his work. He truly did. It had a rhythm and a sense of order that suited him. He was good enough at what he did that the fires he had to extinguish were minimal.

With the mess sorted out, he spent more than an hour on Paris Expressions' branding and marketing. So far, he'd taken them from being called "Today's Fashions," a women's clothing store with a lackluster name and sales to match, to a business with respectable sales. He put his phone on speaker and punched in the store's number. The owner answered on the second ring.

"Evelyn, I want to confirm our meeting today."

"Are you kidding? I wouldn't miss a meeting with my marketing expert unless I were in the hospital. Even then I'd ask to move the meeting there."

Nathaniel could picture the energetic, fiftysomething woman doing exactly that. He grinned. "My guess is that business is up."

Continue reading Falling for Alaska *now!*

About Cathryn

Writing books that are fun and touch your heart

Even though Cathryn Brown always loved to read and had a degree in communications and journalism, she didn't plan to write books. Until one day when she enjoyed a book so much that she wanted to write one.

The book she'd been reading had a bit of fun to it, and that's something Cathryn likes to bring to her books.

She enjoys hiking, sometimes while dictating a book. She also unwinds by baking and reading. Cathryn lives in Tennessee with her professor husband and adorable calico cat.

If there are eight-to-twelve-year-olds in your life, *The Feather Chase*, with the author name Shannon L. Brown, begins her fun mystery series.

Book Discussion Questions

1. Which place in *Crazy About Alaska* would you most like to visit?
2. Is there a place you wouldn't want to go?
3. Would you rather live in an apartment, townhouse, house in a subdivision, or a house on acreage like Adam bought?
4. Have you flown in a small, private plane before? If not, would you like to and where would you like to go?
5. Fresh salmon is one of the joys of an Alaskan summer. Would you rather buy yours in a store or go dipnetting?
6. Holly almost let her past determine her future. Is there a past incident that could have blocked your future?
7. Adam's friend has a cabin that you can't drive to. Is that appealing?
8. Have you had an adventure like their trip to the Swan Lake Canoe Route? Somewhere off the beaten track?
9. Twins would be twice the work, but also twice the joy. If you don't have children who are multiples, do you wish you did? If you are a parent of multiples, share a story about raising them.